"LET THE GODS OF MAN CHOOSE!"

So it was decided and, at the bidding of the elders, Eban and the other young men of the tribe launched themselves into the sky, soaring higher and higher in their efforts to outdo each other and win the hand of the chief's daughter. But first one, and then another and another ended their flights, not wishing to face the threat of the killbird.

Finally, only Eban and Logan hung in the sky daring the wrath of the gods. And, as they knew it must, the killbird came. A white streak appeared and grew behind the killbird as it thundered down upon them. Eban could hear the low rumble of its growl as it neared. *And then the killbird made its choice, and Eban could only dive and pray as the killbird—sleek, deadly, shining—came roaring straight after him. . . .*

More Science Fiction from SIGNET

KILLBIRD

by
Zach Hughes

A SIGNET BOOK
NEW AMERICAN LIBRARY
TIMES MIRROR

To Ray Peekner, Superagent

PUBLISHER'S NOTE

This novel is a work of fiction. Names, characters, places, and incidents are either the product of the author's imagination or are used fictitiously, and any resemblance to actual persons, living or dead, events, or locales is entirely coincidental.

SIGNET TRADEMARK REG. U.S. PAT. OFF. AND FOREIGN COUNTRIES
REGISTERED TRADEMARK—MARCA REGISTRADA
HECHO EN CHICAGO, U.S.A.

SIGNET, SIGNET CLASSICS, MENTOR, PLUME, MERIDIAN AND NAL BOOKS are published by The New American Library, Inc., 1633 Broadway, New York, New York 10019

First Printing, June, 1980

1 2 3 4 5 6 7 8 9

PRINTED IN THE UNITED STATES OF AMERICA

1

On the second day of the second moon of summer I saw the bloodflag hanging limply atop Yuree's hidehouse. A hunter's morning it was, with the mist hanging in the lows. The Lake of Clean Water was there, under the mist. The sun was climbing toward his first leap over the Far Hills.

I had been awake to see the stars die in the early light, to hear the call of the nightbirds as they settled into their secret places, to prepare myself, with water heated over a low fire, using the honed edge of my hardax to scrape away my curse.

I untied the flap of my hidehouse and stood, my face smarting. It is said that not one in a thousand has the curse. I had never known another. For all those beyond the Far Mills who, one in a thousand, suffered, I uttered a prayer to the gods of man. And in the midst of my prayer I saw it, looking up the slight slope to see the couch cover with the almost unnoticeable blood signal. I felt my face burn with a new feeling, not only from the scraping. With my heart pounding I dived back into my hidehouse. The day was not unexpected, had, indeed, been foretold, within half a moon period it turned out, by old Seer of Things Unseen.

Because I was of an early-rising nature, due to my curse, I was the first, waiting outside the hidehouse of Strabo of the Strongarm, my hardax lying atop the pile of buythings. It was not an unimpressive pile, I felt, topped by the well-tanned skins of the swimmers. In addition to the swimmer skins, soft fur for the soft skin of Yuree, there were two handcut buckets of wood filled with the sweetness of the stingers, a pile of god's jewels, two huge skins of the two largest bears ever to be killed by a member of the Strongarm family, and toys carved to please Yuree—females being, at best, somewhat frivolous.

Indeed, I had nothing to be ashamed of, except myself.

I heard movement inside the large hidehouse where Strongarm slept and then the flap was untied and thrown open and I saw the powerful arms which gave our family head his name. Still a young man, Strabo had the eyes of a killer of birds, the legs of a perfect man, the stout, short body of our people. He wore the feathers of a family head with authority, and it was he who had shown the courage to take the family over four ridges into the Valley of Clean Water, thus bringing new prosperity to all.

"I beg to be considered, honorable father," I said, bowing my head.

Strongarm merely glared at me. He had his hardax in one hand, and he extended it, granting me the boon with the traditional motion, but then Strabas was looking past him, her sun-browned skull showing the same delightful shape as Yuree's own lovely head.

"It is only the Haired One, then?" Strabas asked, looking around in disappointment.

"It is early yet," Strabo said.

Even as he spoke I heard movement behind me and turned to see not one but two premen trudging up the slope carrying a pile of buythings. Yuree, daughter of the family head, would receive many offers. I recognized, behind the pile of buythings, Logan, son of Logman. His browned skull gleamed in the light of the early sun, and my heart sank. How could I even dream of being considered when the most handsome premen of the family would be piling their buythings in front of the Strongarm hidehouses?

"Eban of the Hair," Strabas said, watching Logan move closer with obvious approval, "are you not son of the dead Egan the Hunter? And was not his pairmate the daughter of Siltan the Wise?"

"I know the intent of your questioning, honorable mother of us all," I said, bowing my head. "I have talked with the Seer of Things Unseen, and you need have no concern, for it is recorded that my mother, daughter of Siltan the Wise, was not daughter of his loins but prize of battle, thus there is no blood taboo."

"Yes, it is true," Strabo muttered, although it seemed to pain him to say such.

I could not fault the pairmate of our family head for her concern. Inbreeding is the enemy of any family, and the all but starving weaklings of the low slopes are proof of that, mating indiscriminately with no thought of the future.

"Humph," Strabas said, turning her attention to Logan, who placed his buythings carefully and put his hardax, not nearly as good as mine, atop. Logan looked at me and rubbed the top of his head meaningfully, his fingers sliding over the slightly oily surface of his skull. I looked away. My own skull still tingled from its daily scraping.

Now others began to arrive, until, by the time the sun was burning away the mist, there were eleven premen, all unpaired, waiting in front of the Strongarm hidehouse. It was then that Yuree chose to make her appearance. I felt my face burn and knew the pleasant weakness of my knees which I had begun to feel long before she was due to come of age.

She looked at me and smiled, her beautiful skull gleaming with a morning application of oil to protect it from the sun. But her smile, although I felt it was for me alone, was also spread around to encompass Logan,

Teetom his running friend, Young Pallas and the others.

"Is that all, then?" Strabas asked, looking down the slope toward the hidehouses of the family, where morning cookfires were beginning to smoke.

"Is not every eligible preman in the family enough for you?" Strabo asked, patting his pairmate on her well-shaped haunch. "And so, Eban, son of Egan the Hunter, what do you speak?"

"I speak the sweet of the stingers," I said, placing the two buckets of the delicious and sticky stuff at Yuree's feet. "The hides of the swimmers to be soft on Yuree's skin, the hides of the bears, one killed by my father, one by myself. I speak playthings to please, the chewed skin of the deer for nighttime comfort in the cold of the winters. My hardax, the ax of Eban the Hunter, will provide. My hidehouse is new, of the finest skins, and behind it, in the sun, the provisions for winter are drying already."

"Well spoken," Strabo said.

"He speaks not of his hair," Strabas muttered, looking at my skull and my face, where the stubble of my hair made a darkness.

"And Logan, son of Logman, what speak you?" Strabo asked.

Logan's buythings were more numerous, but contained nothing as important as a bearskin. The others were comparable. I was beginning to be sorry I had gone first before it was over, for there was nothing to do but stand and listen as the premen of the family made their offers and their promises. When at last it was over and all had spoken, there was a silence. The females of the family, leaving their cookfires, had begun to gather. I felt as I usually felt when the family gathered, as if all eyes were on me, on my prickly skull, my darkened face, my limbs which were not as strong-looking and beautiful as those of the other premen. My body, too, was somewhat of a curse, although, since I was merely a preman, there was hope. But where Logan, for example, was squat and thick, his arms short and powerful, his legs shorter from the knees down than from the knees up, I was thin, almost as thin as the starving weaklings of the low slopes, and my arms were long, my legs long and slim. It was not that I was not strong. The games proved, to the surprise of all, that my slim arms with their bunched muscles at the bicep were strong, that my long legs, making me a full hand taller than any of my contemporaries, were powerful and, surprisingly, seemingly tireless. It was my legs which were the secret of my success as a hunter, for I could cover half again as much ground in a stride as, say, Logan with his short and beautiful limbs.

But it was time for the selection. Strabo pulled himself erect. "Well spoken, all of you," he said. "You do me and my daughter honor, and the choice will be difficult. You all know the custom. It is for the mother to speak first."

Strabas stood forward. She was dressed in her finest, although the weather was hot for swimmer skins. "It is cruel for me to have but one choice," she said, smiling at the young premen who waited in expectation. "I know you all. I have known your fathers and your mothers and, in some cases, your fathers' fathers. But the custom is the custom, and while I would choose you all, could I but do so, I must harden my heart and choose but one. That one, my choice, is—" She paused, but it was not effective, because we all knew her choice. Even he knew it, for he was shifting from one foot to the other, a proud smile on his face. "—Logan, son of Logman," she said. The assembled females oohed in agreement.

"And now I must choose," Strabo said. He looked up at the sun and made a worship sign. "My pairmate has spoken well, and I, too, regret that by not saying names I exclude some of the finest young premen of the family. But the custom is the custom, even for

Strabo of the Strongarm. I choose Young Pallas and Cree the Kite." As father, Strongarm had two choices.

In actual practice, the custom was not always fulfilled, for if the daughter coming of age was not desirable or rich there would seldom be enough premen to fulfill all of the allowed choices. It was considered to be honorable if two premen applied at a coming of age, shameful if there was only one, so that in some cases buythings were exchanged merely to have at least two applicants. Once, when I was very young, I remember Stillas the Housemaker leading a two-man raid on another family merely to capture one preman to assure his daughter of having two applicants. After the choice was made—the family member, of course—the captured preman was released.

And now there was a pause as Yuree, shy and smiling, stood before us. "My father and mother honor me with their wise choices," she said. "I am the most honored of prewomen. It is not pride which forces me to choose, but the custom, for who am I to question the age-old ways of the family? And so, with humbleness, I choose my three." The way she emphasized the "three" told me that she did feel a little pride, for not many girls had the opportunity to choose three.

"My choices," Yuree said, "are Teetom . . ." I found myself holding my breath. "Yorerie the Butcher . . ." There was an intake of breath, for that choice was a surprising one. Yorerie the Butcher, preparer of meat, always smelly, crude, cursed with a bent of tongue which made speech difficult, was an unlikely choice. But, on the other hand, so was Teetom, the shadow of Logan. Teetom was a mean-natured preman with a hint of cruelty in his makeup, as if to make up for his weakness. He had been a sickly child and, as a result, was stunted, was two hands shorter than Logan.

"And my third choice," Yuree said, as I prepared to pick up my buythings and go back to my loneliness, "is

Eban, son of Egan the Hunter." And as she said it she looked me full in the face, a smile lighting her lips.

Those who had not been selected began to pick up their buythings. When they had gone, Strabo sighed and stood forward.

"And now, as is the custom, the new woman will be given her chance to choose."

It was breath-holding time again, for two things could happen. First, Yuree could make a choice and it was all over. Secondly, she could refuse to make a choice and then it was in the hands of the gods of man.

"May I look first?" Yuree asked, with a charming smile directed at her father.

"Yes, my daughter," Strabo said proudly, pleased that she was wise enough to examine the offerings before making a choice. Many prewomen let their hearts rule and choose without regard for the future or for the ability of their pairmates to provide for them.

Yuree started at the end of the line, with the pile of buythings offered by Yorerie the Butcher, made delighted sounds, pawed through, leaving the pile untidy, and moved on. It was several minutes before she came to my pile, and then I stood as if frozen, afraid to look down, as she knelt and pulled my pile apart.

"Such lovely bearskins," she cooed, and I flushed, hoping, for the first time, that she would choose me immediately. "But," she went on, "Logan's offerings are beautiful, as are those of Cree and Teetom. It is so difficult."

"It is difficult," Strabas agreed, kneeling beside Logan's pile of buythings, "but consider this," she said, holding up a lovely beaded skirt of deerskin.

"There is no need for haste," Strabo said.

Yuree stood, smoothing the tight little skirt of grass over her shapely rump. "It is sooooo difficult."

I knew that she was not going to pick. It was going into the hands of the gods of man. So be it, I said to myself.

"Can you not choose?" Strabas asked, holding up the deerskin skirt.

"No, Mother, I cannot. I am too honored by the offerings of the finest premen of our family," Yuree said.

"She will not choose," Seer of Things Unseen had told me, not a half moon past. "She will extract the last measure of it, sending it into the hands of the gods of man."

And Seer was right.

"We will leave it to the gods of man to choose," Strabo said, with a smile of satisfaction.

"Will you, Yuree, daughter of Strabo of the Strongarm, give a sign, a sign to encourage?" This was Logan.

"I will," she said. She put her hand on her chin. She made such a pretty picture that I felt my knees go weak again. "But I must have time to think. My sign will be suspended from the top of the hidehouse before the sun seeks its rest."

I knew it all, all aspects of the custom. Only two nights past I had sat before the fire of the Seer of Things Unseen and she, sucking the juices from tender meat which I had prepared for her, unable to chew with her toothless gums, had told me once again.

"She will not choose," Seer had said. "And she will demand brave and dangerous things."

For, you see, she had two choices. If asked to give a sign, she could, if she chose, give a hint as to the identity of her first choice and, thus assured, that lucky preman could apply himself to the last tests with confidence. However, she could also choose to forego giving a clue and to demand a task, a test, a gift.

"Eban," old Seer had said. "It is said you have the curse, and yet would your scalp burn in the sun if your curse was allowed to grow?"

Indeed, when I was young and let my hair grow it was unnecessary for me to oil my skull against the summer sun, but curse it was, along with my skinny limbs.

"It is said," Seer went on, "that beyond the far hills are families who do not consider hair as a curse, but as a protection, even an adornment."

"They must be mad," I said.

"Is it not mad to seek danger in order to be considered for the dubious joy of being pairmate to a spoiled child?" Seer asked.

She was talking about the prewoman I loved, had loved for as long as I could remember.

"If a preman cannot face danger for what he desires," I answered, "he does not deserve to be called man."

"She will send some of you to find death," Seer said.

So be it, I thought, as I, having waited the long day through, saw Strabo of the Strongarm come from his hidehouse and reach for the message string, and then I moved closer and watched as he tied on the clue which Yuree was giving us. I saw the other chosen watching, and I saw Teetom's face blanch, he being the first to see as Strabo stepped away. I saw it then. There was no mistaking it. I'd seen it before, on Strabo's father when he was family head, on Strabo himself. The thing which hung there was multicolored, connected by the hard veins, lumpy, hard, beautiful and deadly.

All Yuree was asking her future pairmate to do was bring her a necklace of dragon guts.

2

I spent the night alone atop a dome. God likes chaos. I used my hardax to chop and strew underbrush and a few trees, working in the late-evening light until I had transformed the very peak into a tangle in the center of which I made my bed and lay down with the fire burning low, godsticks in my hands making the sign.

"God of Chaos," I prayed. "I have prepared a small place for use, feeble as I am, unable to wreak the huge and terrible beauty which is in your power alone. I use it to pray to you, to pray to you to guide me into the land of the dragons, to give strength to my arms and courage to my heart."

God sent a sign. I saw it coming from the far horizon, to the west, where the hills were high and the forests deep, from where Strabo had led us to the Valley of Clean Water. It was burning there in the night sky, a star larger than the rest, moving relentlessly toward me but high, high, up there where the gods of man lurk. It moved directly over me and continued until, after a long, long time, it went below the lower hills from which the sun rises to sink, some say, into the field of large water which is there beyond the deadly flats where once, Seer of Things Unseen says, there were giants in the old days.

A sign. God spoke. I rubbed my godsticks and made the sign and fought sleep. I thought of my father. When I was to go on my first hunt he gave me the hardax. Dragonskin. Lovely and deadly and capable of cutting rock. Jagged, laced to the sturdy wooden handle with animal thongs. I had never allowed one spot of the red dragon's blood to stain it, polishing it daily, oiling it with the fat of the swimmers. I had learned early that there is a certain amount of oil in the skin, so on long hunts I rubbed it, being careful of the sharp cutting edge kept keen by constant honing, against me, my face, my belly, my arms. Until it gleamed. No one had a finer hardax. And no one had such a father.

I awoke with the sun and did not scrape my curse. I would be away for days, moons perhaps. There would be no one to see my shame. I ate of the fruit from trees and went down the hill to find Seer of Things Unseen at her cookfire. I gave her a softened and well-cooked piece of deermeat.

"Seer," I said, "it is said that the dragons inhabit the far hills toward the rising sun."

"So you are determined to go," she said.

"I ask your blessing and I beg to be allowed to share a bit of your wisdom, as much as my poor head can absorb."

"You go to find death."

"Perhaps."

"As your father did."

"Then I will live in the memory of men as being brave."

"Ghosts hear no praise," she said. She sighed and coughed. "There be dragons in the far hills. There have always been and there always will be, for brave men such as Egan the Hunter, who last slew a dragon and presented its gaudy guts to the elder Strabo, come but once in a thousand moons."

"You think I am not one of those men?" I asked.

"You are but a child, and a dragon's teeth are sharp, far-reaching and deadly."

"But I am the son of my father, and he slew a dragon."

"And was slain," she said grimly, "by still another dragon."

"I am fleet of foot," I said. "More so than anyone else in the family."

"A dragon's teeth travel with the swiftness of an evil thought," Seer said. "And his eyes are death, searing and blasting and burning."

"I will not allow him to spit his teeth at me nor to catch me in his evil eye," I said, full of the confidence of youth.

"Eban, my son," she said, "don't go. Stay. There are other prewomen. The daughter of Bla the Window looks upon you with interest."

I shuddered. The daughter of the Window was ugly and of shrill voice. Yuree's voice was the coo of the woodland birds.

"Well, there is this," Seer said. "Perhaps you will not find a dragon." She chuckled. "I'm sure the others won't. So perhaps you won't and then it will all be in the hands of the gods of man, foolish as that may be for those who tempt them."

"Perhaps I won't," I said, "but I will try."

"Yes," she said.

"How will I know?"

"When you see the white bones of death, you will know."

No one alive in the family had even seen a dragon. My father had, had slain one, but he was dead. And my mother had died of grief. I left the Valley of Clean Waters, climbing the near ridge to look down and out and up to still another ridge, and for the first few days I walked in fear, expecting to see the white bones of death, sign of a dragon, behind every tree, at the top of each ridge, in the bottom of each valley. I traveled light, my hardax, my sleepskin, a bag of dried meat, for the hills were abundant in summer with fruit and

game large and small. I ate well and drank deeply from
free-flowing springs of cold and delicious water and
made my bed under the trees, looking upward to see
the cold stars and, once, twice, the sign from God, the
glowing messenger which came from the west and
burned fire as it passed over me. I didn't know which
direction the others chose, and I didn't care. Perhaps
Logan would make a serious effort to find a dragon,
perhaps not. I, like the Seer of Things Unseen, had
little confidence in the sincerity of the others.

Many times I had lost myself in the hills, leaving the
family far behind to wander and seek the view from
the next hilltop. Once I traveled as far as the low
slopes, there to see the inbreeders, weak, starving,
fighting among themselves and breaking the basic rule
of God. I had no desire to go among the inbreeders, to
see the blood of man spilled, as they spilled it on the
slightest provocation. How they must breed, to be able
to afford to squander life, God's greatest gift. Not that
I fear them. In my healthful strength I could lift two of
them and toss them headlong, but they are sick with
the ultimate sickness, the madness, and I fear con-
tagion.

I set my course away from the known haunts of the
inbreeders, making my way slowly—seeing places not
before seen by members of my family—toward the unknown hills to the north of the place where the sun
rises, into vast and lonely forests, unaware of the passage of the days, for time was not important. Should
the others come before I returned, the custom demanded a full moon of waiting. And when I returned
with the necklace, and I was determined to do so, it
would be over and the gods of man would be robbed.

There came a day when the hills descended in front
of me and there were high ridges only behind me and I
could see a vista which was strange and forbidding. I
moved slowly, my skins tied high to bare my chest and
belly to feel danger, and there was none. There were

deer and once or twice a distant sight of a bear, tempting me. I denied myself repetition of the test of manhood, killing one of the huge and dangerous animals. Two bearskins awaited me, awaited to decorate and make warm the floor of my hidehouse for my pairmate. A tawny lion stalked me, making the stubble of hair which was growing on my neck crawl with warning, but my shouts scared the animal away. I made note of him, for not since my father's father had a member of the family killed a lion. Killing a lion was on the same order of bravery as collecting a necklace of dragon's guts and almost as dangerous, for my father's father told tales of a lion killing two men while bearing five arrows in his body, one so near his heart that blood pumped out as he moved.

I first sensed danger when I came down a long, sloping hillside, moving cautiously through the trees, which were decreasing in size. I felt it begin to tingle in my chest, and then I bared my belly and wiped away the sweat and I could feel it better, a little warning tingle which made my heart pound. I moved back and came down another way, a mile distant from my first approach to the valley's bottom, and the tingle was so faint I went forward. There, where the tingle originated, I saw a heap of rubble, the stones and strangeness which gave home to the spirits which warned with a tingle in the chest and belly, and I felt very much alone.

There was a stream and then a hill. Beyond the hill, I thought, I could see the deadly flats, and that would be the limit of my travel, for no man goes down into the flats and returns. I climbed the hill, picking my steps with the unconscious silence of the hunter, careful of loose stones. I peeked over the top of the hill and saw a valley stretching before me. I felt no danger. I stood and started walking down the hill and almost stumbled over the bleached white bones of a deer. A jangle of alarm was in my head, and I fell to the ground, rolling quickly to shelter behind a large rock. Cautiously I looked out, and not a dozen steps away there was another pile of bleached bones.

"When you see the white bones of death . . ."

My blood pumped. My face burned. Inch by inch, rock by rock, I eased my way down the hillside. There could be no mistake. The white bones of death were everywhere, some of them old, some so old they were nothing more than white ash. There were no freshly killed animals. Either the dragon had depopulated the area of wildlife or the survivors had learned, through experience, not to walk on that deadly hillside.

Knowing that I had never faced such danger, not even when I stood alone with only my longbow against the giant black bear, I rested, feeling the sun warm my back, willing my heart to stop its wild poundings. My mind did things of its own. I yearned for a running mate, a friend, such as Logan's Teetom, even a Teetom, who in my hour of loneliness could say, "You can do it, Eban. You can do it."

Oh, gods of man, I had been alone so long, so long. When my father failed to return from the hunt and there came a report that he had last been seen heading toward the far hills where there were dragons, I was but a bare-assed learner, running free through the camp, permitted to snatch food from any fire, treated with the sometimes amused but always fond tolerance of all. I mourned for my father, but even then, having been on my first hunt, I had my hardax, and with my father dead, I was the man. I told my mother not to weep, for she had her man. And then the curse came and darkened my skull and nothing that Seer of Things Unseen could do would cause it to go away, and was it grief for my father or shame for me which caused my mother to weaken, to spend her days lying in the hide-house sighing, weeping, and then burning with the fever?

I had never had anyone, since then. Life, of course,

is God's most precious gift, so even an accursed one
was sacred, but there were the taunts from my contemporaries, the laughter behind my back. When it became
evident that I was to be different in other ways the
shame of it pushed me into myself. I set up my hidehouse, legacy of my father, on the far fringe of the
family area, went my solitary way, and in my desper-
ation and unhappiness took chances, bracing the fierce
bear, nearly dying in his clutch as his great heart
pumped out his life just in time to keep his carnal-
smelling maw from closing over my head.

Soon, however, they did not taunt me. Although
striking a fellow man is punishable, certain games, tests
of strength, are encouraged; and soon I was able to
handle my peers with an ease which caused mutterings.
It was no test at all to pin Logan, or Young Pallas, or
even the hulking Yorerie to the ground in a wrestling
match. In games of skill and endurance I excelled, running faster than the swiftest, able to trot for endless
hours to bring a deer to bay and then, his giant carcass
dragging to the ground, to carry the animal back to
camp to turn him over to the family of Yorerie the
Butcher for preparation and sharing. My longbow was
two hands longer than even the longbow of the family
head, Strongarm, and only the respect which I owed to
our family head prevented me, in hand games, from
besting the Strongarm himself.

But I was and had always been alone. There was
only one bright spot in my life, and that was in the
form of a sunny-faced prewoman, Yuree, who, perhaps
in pity at first, came to me and talked to me. She was
so beautiful, her body short and round and soft, her
skull gleaming and oiled, her wide eyes alert as the
eyes of a frightened female deer. Even as a child she
knew her powers, sending me to the top of the tallest
fruit tree to toss down the ripest fruits with no more
authority than her smile.

"Eban," I remembered her saying, as I lay behind

the rock and let my eyes cover the ground in front of me, counting the bleached piles of bones which, it seemed, grew more numerous further down the slope, "what will you do when I come of age?"

"I don't know," I mumbled, not daring to think that I, the freak, the accursed one, could presume to ask for her.

"Oh, you pain me," she said. "Will you not ask for me?"

"Yuree," I said, finding it hard to breath. "Do I dare think you'd want me to ask?"

"Of course, silly," she said, with a teasing smile. "Not that I promise to choose you."

"It will be honor enough to be allowed to ask," I said. "But the daughter of the family head could not be pairmate to a haired one."

"Oh, pooh," she said. "We'll have Seer burn it off."

I wore the blisters for days, after I tried to burn away my curse myself.

And now I could feel the summer sun doing its work on my partially exposed scalp, the hair being by now about a finger long and tawny like the hide of a lion. And was that a noise from below?

And so it was only Yuree with whom I could talk, share my shame, my dreams. When she would sneak away from her hidehouse on a spring night and lie in my arms and allow me to touch her lips with mine, to do all those wonderful and blood-rousing things which prepeople are allowed, her skirt or loincloth tucked securely between her legs to mark the only off-bounds area, I dared to think of it, of her in my hidehouse, with me bringing her the spoils of the hunt, for I was, truly, Eban, son of Egan the Hunter.

"I will dress you in lion skins," I said.

"Oh, will you?" she breathed, her voice made low and funny by my kisses on her bared torso. "Oh, will you?"

"For you I will gather a necklace of dragon guts," I promised.

Ha. I had not remembered that. Was that a sign? So long ago I had promised her. Oh, gods of man, it was. It was a sign. I was the favored one. She had remembered, and the multicolored thing hanging from her father's hidehouse was the sign that it was, actually, unbelievably, Eban who was the favorite.

At that moment I was ready to slay two dragons, three dragons, a dozen dragons, to festoon my Yuree in gaudy and lovely guts. And at that moment I heard a noise behind me and turned to see a tawny shape move swiftly from cover to cover. So it was not only the possibility of a dragon before me. There was the lion behind me, having tracked me, stalked me.

It was a tight situation. If I moved, the dragon's teeth would come spitting to kill me. If I remained behind the rock, I would end up with four manweights of lion on my back. Keeping in shelter, I strung my finest arrow, tipped in dragonskin, to my bow, put my hardax atop the rock ready for use, rolled to my back so that I could watch. The lion was silent, but I caught a glimpse of him as he moved closer. His intentions were clear. I considered running for it, back up the slope, but he was above me and I was at a disadvantage.

The game continued for a long, hot, sweaty period during which the sun moved perceptibly. I listened for sounds from below, for sounds of the dragon. There was nothing. Only the sun and the buzz of insects and the loose rock which rolled down toward me just before the lion coughed, leaped, made his charge, arching high to come down at me from up the slope, his tawny hide shining against the sky. I loosed my best and most deadly arrow and reached for the hardax even as he was airborne, and then he was descending, claws showing from his pads, and my arrow lodged ineffectively in his haunch.

In that swift and instant moment of action I wondered if my father had died thus, at the claws and fangs of a lion instead of in a spitting storm of dragon's teeth. So I was to die, mauled and maimed, food for the lion of the mountains. But then there was a terrible sound, even as the lion began his descent, and I saw his body seem to pause in midair and the life run out of him with blood springing from his head, and then I was rolling to keep his vast weight from landing atop me and he was beside me, jerking out his life.

A sound such as I'd never heard before, a wail of ghostly anguish, high-pitched, whining, came from below. There was a rumble, a hard clanking sound.

Oh, gods of man.

I took one moment to make sure the lion was dead. He looked intact, with only his head damaged, pulped, bloody, but the hide excellent with only the one arrow hole in the flank. I retrieved my arrow and lay beside the dead animal, admiring his magnificent coloring, the powerful and now useless muscles, the yellowish and deadly teeth exposed in a death's-head grin. The sound from below came to a halt.

From directly below there was the bellow of a dragon's voice, and teeth swept up the slope, making leaves dance and fall and sending a shower of dust into my eyes as they struck against the rock which protected me. More frightened than I'd ever been, I waited for the deadly rain to cease. It was said that very old dragons had long since spit out all their teeth and had only their deadly eyes. This, then, was not one of them, although all dragons are ancient.

Silence. I lay there, forcing myself to review everything I'd ever heard around the campfires on the subject of dragons.

By the will of God, dragons did not breed. God help man if they did. By the will of God, dragons stayed on their dragon paths, beaten into hardness by the eternity of their vigilance, for dragons were God's first creations, were on earth before God made man from the fresh, red bones of a bear and made him walk upright, as the bear does on occasion.

What else did I know? The range of the dragon's teeth is limited, and the teeth cannot penetrate rock or a huge tree. The dragon's eyes are deadly at closer range, but can kill only in line of sight, being deflected by trees, stone or, one old man claimed, by a stout shield of animal hide. Dragons protect. What? Only God knows, but it was said that originally the intention was to keep man from leaving the mountains to enter the deadly flats.

So. I was not exactly an authority on dragons, and down there, hidden by the trees, I had me a dragon.

The lion had attracted the dragon's attention, and the sounds I'd heard had been the dragon moving to a point directly below me. I thought about that. It seemed to me that it would be best to get out of there and make a new approach. I began to crawl up the hill, keeping very, very low. In an open area the ground around me suddenly spurted dust and there were deadly snaps in the air. I leaped for a rock, and the teeth crashed against it. Then with one leap I was among the trees, and the teeth thudded harmlessly into the tree trunks.

I made another approach. I went far to the north and came down. There were no bones of death there. The range of my dragon seemed to be limited. I had a bad moment when I saw, overgrown and ruined, something I'd never seen, a dragon's path, dark and eerie, cut by eons of vigilance into the hillside, flat, wide. I hid and waited. Nothing happened. I moved to a vantage point. To the south along the dragon's path there was a huge rock slide, closing off the path. So, I reasoned, the dragon's northward patrol was ended by the slide. I crept toward it, climbed the chaos of the rocks, peered over. The dragon's path continued, and, oh, gods of man, he was there, to the south an arrow's flight, squat, ancient, awesome. His round head in the middle of his squat body was motionless, but even at that distance I could see the gleam of his fearsome eyes. I held my breath, ready to leap down the rock slide if he saw me and came after me.

The path was in better shape on the far side of the rock slide, hard and shiny, with only a few small trees and weeds growing in it. The tracks of the dragon were in the center, and it was well beaten. The path had been cut into the side of solid rock so that a cliff towered above it, ending in a slope of rock topped by the forest. I heard a scream, and the dragon's head turned slowly, the eerie wail creaking into my ears, and then the rumble as he turned and slowly, feet pounding and clanking, came toward me. I lowered myself, peering out between two rocks. He halted halfway to me and went to sleep. There was silence.

I studied the land. Below the dragon's path the slope fell away into a deep ravine, from which I could hear the sound of a stream. Among the trees I could catch glimpses of white bones. To the south, beyond the point from which the dragon had spat death upon the lion, there was another rockslide. The dragon was effectively penned into a section of his path not more than an arrow's flight long.

"Well, Eban the hunter," I said, "it is only to kill him now."

How? That was the question. Once, according to legend, a dragon had been killed by rolling burning logs down on him from above, but my father had slain his dragon in a different way. I looked to the cliff which towered above the dragon's path, highest in the center of the remaining range. I made my plans. It was early afternoon, and I wondered if I would do well to wait for darkness. Could dragons see in the night? We knew so little about them.

Yes, I would await the coming of night. I withdrew, walking fearfully along the abandoned portions of the dragon's path, and made my camp, dined on dried meat and fruits, slept well in spite of what I faced. I awoke, willing myself to do so, with the moon not yet above the hills, and in an almost inky darkness, I made my way to the top of the cliff. The dragon was a dark and foreboding blackness down below. I began to gather rocks, hefting stones as large as I could handle, rolling some into place. Once I dislodged a loose stone and sent it clanking and crashing downward, and the area near me was lit, suddenly, by the fierceness of the dragon's eye, a blinding blaze of light as if from the sun which, as I cowered back into the forest, swept back and forth and then went away.

When the sun sent its warning of morning in the form of false dawn, I had a pile of rocks higher than my head. My hope was that once I dislodged them, pulling away the small log on which they all rested, they would gather their brothers as they rolled down the slope in a growing slide which would bury the dragon and make him immobile.

I waited until the light was good, and it was almost my undoing. For as I readied myself, the dragon, who had been in perfect position, moved, first making that eerie scream, then jerking into motion, his peculiar feet making clanking sounds on the pathway which he had beaten down into hardness with his eons of patrol. He went to the far south and paused. I waited for an hour and was impatient. I steeled myself and stepped out to the brink of the cliff and stood there, my body exposed. Nothing happened. Had he expended his teeth? If so, he still had his eyes. I knew that from the incident of the night. But he had to be moved back to the center of the cliff to be a target for my manmade rock slide.

"Dragon," I said softly. "Come to me. Be a nice dragon and come to be killed."

He didn't hear.

"Dragon," I yelled.

Creak. Clank. I dived for the trees as teeth spattered around me. Well, I had his attention. I could hear him now, clanking, pounding the hard path. He halted below me, and I dared look out. Teeth thudded into the trees above me. And then I saw his eye, the one looking toward me, glow. A lance of fire shot out, bright, hurting my eyes, searing the trees only hands above my head. I tried to dig myself a hole.

Yes, I had his attention.

But he was not quite in the proper position.

I examined him. His tough skin, parts of which would be so wonderful for making hardaxes and other tools, was bleeding. All old dragons—and all were old—bled, their dark blood seeping through the tough skin to redden and blotch. This, I felt, in spite of his supply of teeth, which seemed to be endless, was a very old dragon, blood-spotted almost everywhere except in his gleaming eyes.

I wanted him to move. I threw a branch, and a lance of fire caught it in midair, and he moved, just as I wanted him to. Dragons, I decided, were not too smart. He was directly below my pile of rocks, and I rolled quickly, kicked the log, and it went bounding down the cliff, followed by a growing rumble as my rock pile fell and, as I'd hoped, gathered force and went sweeping down in a cloud of dust and a rumble like summer thunder. And over it there was the creaking and clanking as the dragon tried to avoid the oncoming mass. I watched, fascinated and praying to my gods, and then the first stones were upon him, making hard sounds as they glanced off his hard skin, and then the force of it hit him and I saw him tilt and I heard the rattle of his teeth flying everywhere with his eyes flashing and then he was going over and the rocks piled up on him, crushing him, imprisoning even his huge strength under many, many manweights of rock and dirt. All was silent. The echo of the roar of the landslide faded. I waited. Then, heart in mouth, I began to make my way down the fresh dirt and exposed stones of the cliff, and I lived, did not feel the blasting shock of his teeth or the searing flame of his eyes.

He was almost completely covered. He was on his side, and even in his extremity he tried to kill me, sending out his teeth, rattling them against the stones which covered him, blasting and smoking the stones with the force of his eyes. I waited and watched his death struggles, and it was half the day before he ceased to try to burn his way out of the pile of rubble with his eyes.

The rocks were hot to the touch, and I had to wait for them to cool. Finally, in the early evening, I neared, coming up on his weak side, his exposed belly. He spat one last burst of teeth and then was silent.

By nightfall, I had his belly exposed, being careful not to move the rocks which kept his head from turning. His huge, flat, continuous feet were moving slowly, grinding away at nothing. I was careful to avoid them.

I kept remembering little things. "The dragon's belly is his weakest part," my father had told me.

And so it was.

Still, breaching that belly took the better part of two days, during which I nearly ruined my hardax, put bruises and cuts on my hands, sweated, cursed, tugged, banged away with large stones. I was attacking a plate on the dragon's skin much like the plate on a turtle's belly, and his bones were hard and tough. When at last I had one edge of the plate lifted slightly, I was able to force a branch into the rift to use as a lever. With all my strength I heaved, and one by one the bones gave and then the plate clanged off to ring against the stones and the hard pathway.

Inside were wondrous things. Huge, horned arteries, which I attacked with my poor, mutilated hardax. When I cut through one of them the dragon spat fire at me and the feet stopped grinding away.

I cut more arteries and small veins and began to

gather them, the small veins, because they were indestructible and invaluable for tying things together, for fishing lines, for decoration, since they came in various colors. Soon I had a pile of treasures and was busily cutting my way deeper and deeper into the dragon's entrails. I cut a different kind of artery, and ichor or something similar jetted out. I got some of it on my hands and expected it to burn, but it was cool and slick. I tried to wipe it away. It was oily, like the extract of fat swimmer meat. I wished for something to catch it in, but I had nothing. It would have been invaluable for oiling skulls, for those who were lucky enough not to be cursed.

But the true treasures were still beyond my reach after three days of hard and frustrating labor, and it was not until the fourth day that I found what I sought. I had cut and ripped my way into the entrails of the now thoroughly dead beast, and there were wonders. A store of teeth, long, hard, shiny. I took several, although they were heavy. And then the guts, the gaudy little pretties. They were in several boxlike compartments, all connected in a wondrous way, but the veins connecting them were small and flexible and it was the work of mere hours to collect enough to make a dozen necklaces. They came in various sizes, and different colors, with the little veins sticking out both ends, and I bent the veins together to form a huge multistrand necklace and stood atop the dead dragon, the token of my victory around my neck, sweating, bleeding from accidental contact with sharp points of dragon's skin, and sang my victory song.

I had only two more chores before going home in triumph. I searched the dragon for a suitable piece of skin to replace my mutilated hardax. I found a small plate and used up the remaining edge of my old hardax to cut the bones holding it. Honed and ground and shaped, it would make a beautiful hardax. Then I bundled all the treasure I could carry into my sleepskin and rolled rocks to hide the carcass of the dragon. There was much treasure left. I would return, with all of the men of the family, and strip the carcass, making the family of Strabo of the Strongarm the richest family of the mountains. We could trade for buythings with every family within trading distance.

And one thing else. The carcass of the lion. I was fortunate. The threat of the dragon's teeth had, apparently, kept away the small carrion eaters and even the flying eaters of the dead. The lion was swollen, and when I began to skin him he stank dreadfully, but his skin was intact.

The extent of my triumph was just beginning to hit me. Not only dragon's guts, but a lionskin. The name of Eban the Hunter would live forever in the memories of my people.

Well, to this day I don't know whether it was worth it, skinning a long-dead lion. Stench? Gods of man! I soaked in the first stream I crossed for hours and it was still with me, wearing off, but lingering on the skin, as I made my way homeward, singing my victory song as I went.

3

They heard me coming. The small children were out first, laughing and pointing at me, for I had not scraped my curse and it was finger-long on my skull and finger-joint-long on my face. I paid them no mind. Then there were the women, some calling my name. Old Seer, hobbling from her hidehouse, her toothless mouth contorted in a welcoming smile.

I had my treasures hidden under my sleepskin.

"Logan brought a bearskin," a small boy shouted at me.

"Logan is brave," I said. Gods of man, I was confident.

"What have you got?" the lad asked, trotting along beside me. "Besides hair?"

"You will see, small one," I said.

There was a gathering in front of the hidehouse of Strabo. I went there, beginning to wonder if I should not have halted long enough to scrape away my shame, but my hardax was ruined and I had not had time to hone an edge on my new one.

"So," Strabo said, scowling. "You have returned at last. What speak you?"

"Am I not the last?" I asked.

"You are."

"Then I ask to be heard last," I said.

Seer of Things Unseen was seated in the shade, making rhythm on a hollowed log. They spoke, in the order of their return. Teetom, first, had only swimmer

27

skins. He said he had searched for dragons for a moon
and they were extinct. Yorerie had skins and jewels of
gods, some oblong and red. And so it went. There was
a restlessness. It was known by one and all that they
did not matter, that the decision was to be between Logan and, perhaps, the Haired One.

And then came Logan, with his right leg bandaged,
healing slowly, limping. The bear had reached him
with its fearful fangs. He spoke well and bravely. In
addition to the bearskin, he had flint. As he spoke,
Strabas, mother of my beloved, smiled in approval.

And now, at last, it was my turn.

While the others talked, and all eyes were on them, I
had arranged my treasures, keeping them hidden under
my sleepskin.

"How speak you, Eban the Hunter?" Strabo asked.

"I have fared well," I said. "My honorable father, I
ask your permission to spread my boon among the
family."

"Is it so rich, then?" Strabas asked, greed in her
eyes.

"Rich enough for all," I said.

"Permission," Strabo granted.

"First," I said, pulling out the lionskin, "a special
gift for Yuree, to warm her, to pleasure her, to give her
honor."

There was a collective gasp, and the women
crowded forward to finger the lionskin. I made no
haste, willing to savor the moment, thinking of even
greater triumph to come. I had planned it so carefully.
I didn't know, then, that I was simply stupid to think
that I could buy their love and respect. Oh, they accepted my gifts. They accepted them.

"And now," I said, "for the hunters, for the men of
my family . . ." I reached into my pile of treasures
and brought out the prearranged veins of the dragon
and, with gasping and speculation, distributed one
length to each man of the family.

"A dragon?" Strabo asked, his eyes wide.

"I have not forgotten the family head," I said. "My father presented your father with the tribe's greatest treasure. I can do no less than match his generosity." So saying, I pulled out a necklace of dragon's gut, a match for the one my father had given the elder Strabo. I hung it around Strabo's neck. He beamed and fingered it. The family was hooting in rhythm with Seer's beats. The sounds hung in the still summer air. I glowed with pride.

"Is there nothing, then, for me?" Yuree asked, pouting.

"Be patient," I begged. "For the mothers of the family, each one, and for my friend, Seer of Unseen Things . . ." I brought them out one by one. One gaudy dragon's gut for each woman, three for Seer, who was the oldest.

"You buy your death," she whispered. I grinned confidently at her. The three dragon's guts looked good on her stringy neck.

"And now," I said, facing Yuree. "My greatest pleasure is to present the beautiful and desirable Yuree, and I pray that she will accept and honor me by choosing me, with . . . this."

Women cried out, began to scream and yodel in rhythm, for I held out and then put around Yuree's neck the greatest and most beautiful necklace ever seen. It was three strands thick and hung to her waist, and she went red with pleasure and smiled at me.

"And as a further gift," I shouted, over the din of the women's singing, "I have the carcass of the dragon well hidden, waiting for all the men in the family to gather treasure, to make the family of Strabo the Strongarm the richest in the mountains."

"Honor to Eban the Hunter," Seer said.

"Honor, honor," the women chanted. "Honor to Eban the Hunter, slayer of dragons."

"It is honor to me," Strabo said, kneeling in front of me.

A family head had not kneeled to a man since Strabo's father knelt to pay honor to my father. I put my battered hardax on Strabo's shoulder.

"The honor, honorable father, is shared," I said. "And I renew my pledge to serve you and the family. I do this with great joy."

He rose. There were tears in his eyes. "Had I a son like you . . ." he said.

"If it be God's will, I will be your son," I said.

"Yes," he said. "It is time." He turned. The chanting died. "My daughter," he said. "You have seen. You have heard. Will you now choose?"

Yuree opened her mouth. I saw it form that beautiful word, yes. But it was not to be.

"We have not as yet been assured that the gods of man approve," Strabas said, stepping between me and Yuree.

"Woman," Strabo said, "the choice is Yuree's."

"No," Strabas said, "it is the custom. The mother has the right of last appeal to the gods."

There was a muttering. I'd never heard that one. Neither, apparently, had Strabo. He turned to Seer of Things Unseen.

"It is true," Seer said, shaking her head. "The right was last exercised in the time of your father's father, but it is the custom."

"So be it," Strabo said.

Did Yuree have a look of regret on her face?

"With the dawn, then," Strabo said. "If none of you needs more time for preparation."

Now, sometimes customs can be silly. I felt a great pity for the others, for the likes of Young Pallas and Teetom and Yorerie. They were out of it. Everyone knew it. Everyone knew that if Strabas hadn't spoken up, claimed her last appeal, Yuree would have chosen me and the gods could have gone on sleeping in their high places. Now, because an old woman did not want a haired one for a son, we all faced them, those sleek and fatal gods.

Yet, because of custom and honor we went to our hidehouses and began to take out the birds, stored so carefully, the thin membranes of scraped hide, the tiny but strong lengths of hollowed wood. Because no pre-man could refuse, having gone so far, six of us would dare the displeasure of the gods of man in the light of a summer dawn.

It is said that God gave man wings in a moment of weakness and, realizing it, then placed limitations upon man. And, the limitations being not enough, He then placed the gods of man in the heights to limit man's forbidden pleasure, his escape from the surface of the earth to be limited by his fear of retribution, by his weight, by the vagaries of wind and air. And yet the right to wings was man's from the time he could scrape skins. Only fools, however, abused that right. Wings were reserved for splendid and ceremonial occasions, and the flights were a hymn of praise to the God who loves chaos.

I had flown last during the festival of the new growth, when the crops were peeking out of the ground, and we flew, the young ones, to praise God and to beg for the rains and the gentle sun. And now I would fly for another reason, the best reason I'd ever had.

And, moreover, instead of the brief and swiftly fin-ished hop from a small hilltop in a hidden valley, se-cluded from the eyes of the gods of man, I would fly from the dome upon which I had built my fire, created my chaos, prayed to God before I went to slay the dragon. And beside me would be five others, risking all, some of them, all of them save myself and Logan, for nothing. For from that dome, high above the sur-rounding hills, there was no protection from the eyes of the gods of man. The gods of man would look down, see, select, and choose to speak or remain silent.

What was it in me which prevented me from scraping my shame on that night of all nights? Pride? Was I so sure of my manhood, having slain a dragon, that I no longer feared the disapproval which comes to a haired one? I have learned, since, that pride is a sin against the God of chaos. I spread my wings and oiled them carefully, making the very thin membrane soft and pliant. I reinforced the riggings with the veins of the dragon, making mine the strongest wings of all. I spread them and rigged them, and they arched up. I tried the saddle, and it was soft and comfortable, and, with the wings ready, I prayed, rubbing my godsticks, until the village was quiet. Then I slept to waken to the happy and excited cries of the young ones as they anticipated the glorious day when six sets of wings would adorn the sky at once and fly high, not in a sneaking hop from a low hill.

God made man smaller than the deer, so that his body weight could be lifted by the wings. With so much pre-planning, then, how was his gift of wings so frivolous? If he had not meant man to fly he would not have given him wings, and that was a puzzle, for the gods of man, the killbirds, always waited. Man never knew, even on a short and secretive flight, when God would be angered and send His messenger flashing down from the skies.

Never before had I felt His presence so vividly as I carried my wings to the dome, Young Pallas trudging along behind me, Logan in front of me.

The men were working atop the dome, clearing a path for takeoff. There was feasting and singing. I passed nearby Seer, and she touched my arm. "Oh, Eban, it is not too late," she said.

"She is the daughter of a family head," I said.

Pride. My pairmate-to-be deserved the test. The last time a mating had been put into the hands of the gods of man was during the lifetime of Strabo's father, when Strabo's younger sister had come of age and was sought not only by men of the family, but by men of an adjoining family from whom our family had since been separated by distance, thanks to the inspired move by Strabo of the Strongarm. Yuree deserved the best, and without the ultimate test of courage, without the approval of the gods of man, she would not be getting it.

I regretted, momentarily, that Yuree was not on the dome to see the takeoff. But it made sense. She was far away, down the long slope, in the valley, at a distance of the walk of a four fingers' movement of the sun. There she could greet the victor, the final choice. I could almost feel her arms around me.

"May the killbirds be sleeping," Seer said, as I left her.

"Are there any who would withdraw, without malice?" Strabo asked.

As he expected, as demanded, no one spoke. Teetom was white of face as he fussed with his wings.

"You know the custom," Strabo said. "He who flies longest, who tempts the gods longest without destruction, is the victor."

"We know," Yorerie said, in his thick-tongued way.

We all knew. We knew that once we had cleared the ground there was no dishonor in ending the flight as quickly as we chose. In fact, honor came to the man who landed first, for he did not continue to risk a precious life. But I was not after honor. I had honor, more than any man in our family. I was after Yuree, and to win her I would fly to the low clouds, to the dim blue of the high places, into the lair of the gods of man, the killbirds, themselves.

But there was a look of determination on the face of Logan, too.

"May the killbirds be sleeping," Strabo said, making a gesture with his hardax. There was a low, mourning chant as we poised there in a line, standing in the cleared runway with our hearts pounding, looking forward to that glorious freedom of flight and fearing it at the same time, none of us knowing who would be chosen by a streaking killbird.

Above us there were soft little white clouds and vast areas of blue sky. Clouds would not have helped, for killbirds see through them.

"God have sympathy," Strabo said, as we began running. Then the ground fell away under my feet and I leaned and felt the wings bite into the air and experienced the giddy happiness of leaving the ground with the trees brushing my feet before my wings caught hold and lifted me. Below I could see Teetom's wings tumbling as his feet dragged a treetop and he was out of it. The first. Five of us left. Logan above me and Yorerie, yelling a crazy song of happiness, by my side.

"Ha, Yorerie," I called, trilling the words.

"Ha, Eban," he trilled back. And then he was off on a wind, lifting, and I felt the same uplift and soared, the green trees growing smaller below me, the valley coming into my view. I soared to within a few wing lengths of Yorerie. Below I could see Cree the Kite landing in a hillside clearing. Two down with honor. I looked up. The sky was clean. No telltell track of whiteness to speak of the thunder of a killbird.

"Ha, Yorerie," I called. "Go down, for even should you win she will exercise her last appeal and reject you."

"Ha, Eban," he called, laughing, speaking more clearly than I'd ever heard him speak. "I care not. I have known I would be rejected, but I fly."

Oh, the fool. He had been in it all along merely for the chance to risk a long and soaring flight.

Young Pallas wisely went in at the grassy side of the stream, three arrow flights from the dome. Three down. Logan high above me, soaring, circling. The fool. He was going to make a real contest of it, and with Strabas in his favor would Yuree have the strength to reject him should he win?

I found a rising wind and rode it, circling. We were being foolish. We should have gone in a straight line for the finish point, a meadow in the center of the valley. Instead we circled and soared, riding the hot breath of the valley, warmed by the sun, and above us the trackless sky posed a deadly threat.

Fobs, later known as the Fool, defied the gods. Defied tradition. Defied the advice of his elders, flying his wings without occasion, for his own pleasure, defying God one time too many, as we all watched, we young ones. The killbird appeared, high, first as a streak of white and then as a gleaming dot which sped downward with the speed of lightning, and the great blast left nothing but a rain of debris and tatters of scraped skin from Fobs' wings.

"Yorerie, for God's sake, go down," I yelled, as I circled close.

My eyes were searching the sky. We had been aloft forever, it seemed, much too long, long enough for a killbird to see, to come, to blast.

"Yah, yah, yah," Yorerie yelled, banking, sweeping away so gracefully that it caused a knot in my throat. I dared not leave the rising current of heated air, for Logan was still above me.

Yorerie was skillful. He soared back to within a wingspan of me. "Let us both go down," he said. "For she will reject your hair."

"No," I said. "She will not."

"I go," he said, dropping away, arrowing away toward the meadow. I saw him make his landing, standing, keeping his precious wings from damage. And then it was just the two of us, Logan above me. I began to try to soar to his level, seeking the turn of air which would lift me. When I was near, he laughed.

"Go down, Haired One," he said. "You seek death or rejection."

"Would it please you, living with the knowledge that it was her mother who chose you?" I asked.

"I don't care who makes the choice," he yelled, "so long as I am chosen."

"Let the gods of man decide, then," I said grimly, sweeping away from him so that when the killbird came we would be far apart, leaving the gods of man a choice.

"So be it," he yelled after me.

They were sleeping, I felt, for we had been in the air so long, so long. Fobs the Fool had not flown so long on his fatal flight. Surely the killbirds were sleeping, or God was sympathetic. Surely Logan would know fear. Surely he would go down so that I could go, after him, to claim my prize.

From far below I could hear yelling. "Come down, come down."

We were drifting slowly back toward the dome, circling, gaining height on the column of warm air, and I dreamed that there were no killbirds and man could fly at his pleasure and seek new height and extend the delicious feeling of being free forever.

I did not see the telltale streak of white. I heard the screaming from the ground and then looked up, around, and there, high, near the sun, I saw it, the streak. We were high above the dome. It would be close, for the killbird traveled swiftly, if we tried, now, to reach the safety of the ground, to hide beneath the trees.

"There," I yelled, pointing with my head. He saw it.

"Oh, God," he cried.

"Will you go down?" I yelled.

"Let the gods of man choose," he said.

"Fool, fool," I cried.

He seemed to be frozen with terror, but he was determined. He was set in a circle, riding the column of air. I yelled, "Break out of the circle. Take action."

He seemed not to hear me, and, above, the white

streak grew and grew behind the killbird as he thundered down. Then I could hear the low rumble of his growl, and I, death not being my object, took action, swooping away from the circling Logan. I aimed for the dome with the intent of going into the depression behind it, putting the bulk of the hill between me and the streaking, roaring killbird while Logan was still circling. I tried to extend the line of the killbird to estimate if he had chosen one of us as a target. It was too far up to tell.

I could see the family, at least half of them, Strabo, Seer, all the others, on the dome below me, their faces uplifted, fingers pointing to the death which streaked out of the sky. I had put considerable distance between me and Logan. He still circled. And then it became apparent as the line behind the killbird jogged and the roaring sounded ever louder, the killbird coming so fast that he left his growl behind him, that he had selected and, instead of the relatively stationary target offered by the circling Logan, he had chosen me.

So be it, I said. But I was not ready to give up. I dived with the roar in my ears, the killbird a distinct thing now, sleek, deadly, shiny, the sun reflected off his skin, his deadly nose pointed directly toward me.

I dived toward the dome. Wind sang in my ears, put fierce strain on my frail wings. They would break and I would tumble into the trees. But they held, and I flashed over the dome so low that I could see the teeth in Strabo's mouth as he yelled at me and the roar was in my ears and the killbird was so near I could make out the marking of his skin. Then I was over the dome and diving, and below me was a valley. To put the hill between us, that was my intent. Then the killbird would soar past and be unable to change directions so swiftly to pursue me into the valley, where I would land, in the trees, and lose, for Logan was still high, circling. And then I was past and diving fast while my wings protested and behind me there was a great blast which seized me and lifted me, stopping my dive, throwing me forward. I fought for control. I was alive and the killbird had done his worst and I would climb again and outlast Logan and all would be right with the world. Then I felt something splat against my legs and looked down to see a piece of human flesh, navel clearly visible, slide off my legs, leaving very red blood, and I screamed, looked back, having gained control, to see the top of the dome leveled.

All dead. Strabo. The Seer of Things Unseen, half of the family. I had led the killbird directly to them. I turned, hot tears in my eyes. The top of the dome had become the chaos pleasing to God. Trees blasted, stumps burning, a glint of killbird skin, a huge hole. No sign of people, except a severed leg in a damaged treetop.

Oh, God. Oh, God.

So many lives. So many precious and irreplaceable lives. Half the family. The family head. My old friend, my only friend, Seer.

Logan was streaking for the meadow. I watched him go. Finding the column of air, I soared. I looked up.

"Come," I cried. "Come, killbird. Take me. For I do not want to live."

The killbird's white trail was wisping out, becoming indistinct. The blue sky was empty.

I considered diving down, straight down, to smash into the rocks, but that was a sin which I did not need. Having been responsible for so many deaths, I did not need to extend my time in the burning place by taking my own. I dared not tempt God further. For to seek death would be to rob Him of His right to judge, to punish.

I knew the first taste of that punishment already. I had lost. I was the last one in the air, but I had lost everything. For I had killed the father of the one I loved, and she was now so far beyond my reach that there was no hope. For our customs are the things of survival, and to condone what I had done would unravel the very threads of our means of survival in a world of chaos. I could not even go back. As a bringer of death I was the most abhorred thing in man's world. Yuree. Yuree. How I loved you.

"Come, killbird," I begged. "Please, God, take me. Punish me. Free me from my sadness."

The cold blue sky was empty. I strained my eyes, climbing higher and higher, riding the updrafts. I was drifting away from the valley of my people. The Lake of Clean Water far below was beginning to disappear as hills intervened.

Looking back, it was a glorious flight, but I was in no condition to enjoy. I merely flew there, higher and higher, begging God to send a killbird that never came. I was moving toward the far hills to the east, to the place where I, in my youthful arrogance, thought that I had gained the world merely by slaying a dragon. And in the end I had to come down, for the updrafts deserted me, and I considered crashing into rocks or trees, but again that was taking God's prerogative. I landed in a little clearing, far from the valley of my people. I respected my wings, folding them. I lay in the grass and willed myself to die.

The mind might wish death, but the body never does. It rebelled, after God only knows how long, and I found myself seeking food from the fruit trees, drink from the clear stream.

I had nothing, only my wings. It was chill. I covered myself with grasses for warmth, and by morning I had decided that God wanted me to live. What I would do with my life was now in God's hands. I packed my wings. If a man is to live he must have tools. I carried the wings to the place of the dragon and took what I could with my bare hands. I found a very unsatisfactory piece of dragon skin which I honed for days until it was ready to mount, using dragon veins, to a crude handle. I made a longbow and strung it with dragon veins, fashioned arrows from wood, tipped them with crude pieces of dragon skin. Then I could hunt for meat, and life became an endless series of days, meaningless days. I used the dragon for my house, sleeping in the cavity which I had cleared out.

Many times I wondered about Yuree. The summer days began to grow short, and I set about making myself warm skins for winter. I was alone. I built a hide lean-to to cover the cavity in the dragon and gradually began to build up a winter's supply of sun-dried meat and nuts from the trees. And then, with the first chill of the coming winter putting a coating of frost on the bleeding skin of the slain dragon, I contemplated spending the long winter nights alone in a dead dragon, and there was something akin to panic in me.

I still wished only to die. I could not die. God apparently wanted me to live and to suffer. To seek death was a sin. But perhaps there was a way.

I stood one day with the chill of the winter kissing my back and gazed out toward the flats. It was taboo to go there, but it was a sort of . . . well, I guess you could say common-sense taboo, with no punishment other than danger and death involved. I mean, it was not a sin for me to go there but it was foolish. No man ever went into the flats and came back alive. But wasn't that what I wanted? And to find death there would not be a sin, merely foolishness. Moreover, if God wanted me to live and suffer he could keep me alive in the flats to suffer there, couldn't he?

I could not face winter alone in that dragon's hide. I sought out the highest ridge overlooking the distant undulation of rolling hills which led to the lows and assembled my wings. I took only my hardax and my longbow. Their additional weight would slow my flight, but would not make it impossible.

I waited for a warm day with a wind from the hills behind me. The distant valley shimmered with heat. I ran, leaped, and flew. I used the updrafts. I used all my skill. I was tempting the gods of man, and I didn't care. And they didn't care about me, for no killbird came to blast me into forgetfulness.

At the center of the valley I felt, on my exposed belly, the warning, the tingling. And down there were the piles of stone and other things which, legend says, were the homes of the giants. Shivering, I almost wished there were giants, giants who could squash me with a fist and put an end to it. I flew away from the source of the warning tingle, however, and cleared a ridge, found an updraft on the other side, rode it to clear another ridge.

I suppose it was an epic flight, the longest man has ever made. It extended for half a day, over ridge after ridge as the land dropped away under me until, in the late afternoon, the winds and the updrafts failed me and I sank slowly downward, into a flatness which, after living my life among the mountains, seemed sinister and eerie.

I took a good look as I went down. The land was mostly barren, with rocks exposed, the dirt a dirty red. Far away there was a line of trees which seemed to mark a stream, but they were stunted and unhealthy, unlike the trees of my mountains. I landed running, stumbled over a rock, went tail over wings and smashed the delicate bracings. It didn't matter. I would have no use for wings in this flat desert. I was not hurt. God was looking out for me, keeping me alive to suffer. I salvaged some dragon's veins from the wings and set off toward the distant trees. There was a little rabbity type of animal there in the flats, existing on God knows what, and I killed one with an arrow, skinned him, smelled him, found him to be unsavory but edible. I carried the carcass to the tree line and found a stream of reddish water which tasted tepid. I used my hardax and a piece of flint for a fire and settled in.

I awoke with a feeling of eyes upon me. I leaped to my feet, clutching my hardax. I saw them then. There were three of them. Two men and a woman, the woman lank of body, thinner than I, and with a filthy mane of hair on her skull. The men were equally sorry, with hair on face and head. They were dressed in tattered and filthy skins, and their eyes were sunken into their faces.

"Who are you?" I asked.

"Who are you?" one of the men asked. His words were distorted but understandable.

"I am Eban the Hunter," I said.

"What do you hunt?" the woman asked, licking her lips.

"I have hunted bears and lions," I said, with a swift pride which soon faded as I remembered.

"This is no bear," one of the men said, pointing to the remains of the rabbity animal which had been my meal.

"If you are hungry, eat," I said.

The man leaped toward the carcass and began to tear it with his hands, the other two pushing and yelling, trying to grab a bit for themselves. It sickened me. I stepped forward and pushed one of the men. He was frail, and he fell to his back. The other scrambled away on his hands and knees. Only the woman remained, the food clutched in her hands.

"There is enough for all," I said. I took the animal and cut it into pieces with my hardax, handing each a share. "Eat," I said.

"You are great and mighty," the woman said. "I will be your ——" She said a word which is sometimes used, with shame, by young boys trying to shock. I turned red.

"You like I be your ——?" she asked.

"No," I said harshly, "nor do I want to hear such language."

"I will cook for you and tend your fire, then," she said.

"As you will," I said. "I will sleep."

"Yes," she said. "Sleep. I will stay awake and keep the fire for you."

The two men huddled together and seemed to go to sleep. I curled up and closed my eyes, opening them now and then to look at the woman. Her clothing was mere tatters, showing her long flanks and the curve of her breasts. I slept.

Later in my life I saw men, if the inbreeders deserve the name, seek death by their own hands. But a real man, however sure he is that life is not worth living, clings to life with all his strength, even as his mind wishes ease in eternal sleep. I had a feeling, perhaps not fully realized, that if death was all I sought it would come to me as a pleasant surprise in my sleep that night. So that urge, that sacred will to live, kept my hand on the handle of my crude hardax. A good hunter, it is said, sleeps with one eye open. I'm sure that both my eyes were closed, but there was something in me which was vigilant, for I woke and rolled with one movement and the dragonskin head of my own arrow plunked into the ground where I had lain. It was, on my part, instinctive, I suppose, for if I had been fully aware I would not have done as I did, leaping with one fluid movement to vault the dying fire and shed the blood of the man who had seized my longbow and used it to try to kill me. His skull split with an ease which made it difficult for me, as he fell, to remove my hardax from it. And then I was whirling to meet a new threat as the dead man's companion screamed in rage and, using both hands, tried to break my skull with a huge rock. As it was the rock struck me a glancing blow on the shoulder, numbing it, but it was my eating hand, not my hunting hand, and I swung the hardax, driven by anger at the betrayal—I had, after all, shared my food with them—and by the instinct of survival. The ax flashed in the dying light of the fire and took the second inbreeder on the side of the throat, sliding across bone to sever the large artery there. His life pumped away as he dug futilely in the barren red dirt with his broken and dirty nails. I turned to the woman, who was crouching on the ground, my ax held high.

"Please, please," she cried. "I wanted to warn you, but they would have killed me."

"Is this the way your people reward hospitality?" I asked.

"We have eaten nothing for three suns," she whimpered. "Do not kill me. I will be your ———" That word caused me to curl my lips in disgust.

And then I was struck by the sure knowledge that I had taken life. To be sure, I examined the men. The first, his skull cracked, was surely dead, and the second was gasping out his last breath. I saw the gleaming bone of the skull and was struck by its fragility. The skulls of my people are thick and strong and protect the mind. The inbreeder's skull was thin, so thin. No wonder my ax buried itself in it.

Dead. Men dead at my hand.

I fell to my knees and thrust my face into the dry red dirt. I wailed. I prayed the prayers of the dead. The woman sat, chewing on one dirty fingernail, watching me.

"Are you driven mad, then?" she asked, as I raised my face, now streaked with my tears and the red earth. "Will you kill me?"

"I have had enough of killing," I said. "Do you not mourn your dead?"

"I do not mourn *them*," she said.

I found grass and dead sticks for the fire, no longer interested in sleep. I dug holes with my ax and buried the two men. The earth was hard and the work long, and when it was finished the sun was a redness to the east.

"They took me away from my village," the woman said. "Come there with me and I will cook for you."

I wanted no part of them. But she looked weak and

helpless in the morning light. I told her to remain. I walked about and shot a rabbity animal and cooked it over the open fire. She devoured half of it greedily and carried the remainder in the folds of her filthy skirt. I had made my decision.

"I will take you to your family," I said.

She led the way downstream, and there was a little pitiful growth of woodlands into which she ran, leaving me behind. I followed, and soon I could hear the sounds of young voices, and around a bend in the trail I saw a collection of sorry structures built of grasses, mud, sticks and odd-looking things which I did not recognize. The woman was standing in a clearing on the edge of this collection of shacks, waving to me to hurry. But as I neared I felt the voice of the spirits on my belly. I paused, turned, finding that the warning came from the village. I shook my head and called out to her. She came.

"Do you not feel it?" I asked.

"I always feel hunger," she said. She held out the greasy remains of her breakfast. "Come to my home and I will cook for you and be your ——"

"Fool," I said. "There is warning here."

"Warning?"

"Death."

"Some die," she said, shrugging.

"All die," I said. "I go."

She burst into tears. "Please, please," she begged.

"There is warning, and to ignore it is slow death by the sores and fever."

"No. There is no sickness. Not since the cold of winter."

"I go."

"Take me with you."

"I travel fast and alone."

"You are strong. I am weak. I have no one since the death of my mate."

"You will find another of your kind."

She looked at me in puzzlement. "Of my kind? Are you not of my kind?"

I shuddered. "No."

I turned. She stood there, weeping. She was slim, as I was, and in spite of her personal filth and the dirty, tattered skins she wore, she was woman, a pretty picture when I was not close enough to see the dirt under her fingernails and the scaling of unwashed skin. For a moment I considered taking her. I would not be alone. But my path led eastward. I had no right to add another's life to my foolish risk.

To put distance between myself and temptation, I broke into a ground-eating trot, aiming for a distant line of low hills where there were trees. Twice I had to detour, once around an immense area of God's chaos where the warning was strong and again past a smaller area. By nightfall I was climbing the long slope to the hills and found there a stream. I had eaten nothing all day. I tested the water, and it was silty but clean. I drank deeply, removed my skins, washed them, spread them on a bush to dry, sank myself into the water, snorting, washing my hair and my skin, rubbing it until it glowed with the sand from the stream's bottom. Refreshed, I built a fire and listened to the night noises. Hunger came to me. I heard rustlings in the undergrowth and, with little effort, captured an ugly small furred animal with a long tail. Skinned, he was fat. I cut away most of the fat and cooked a haunch over the fire and was settling down to a not very satisfactory meal when I heard noises. First the unskilled walking sounds of a man unused to being in the forest at night, then the unmistakable sound of a woman weeping. I knew immediately who it was, but I sat quietly. The sounds approached. She saw the fire and came running.

"I have no one," she said, sobbing.

I handed her meat. She ate, heedless of the dripping onto her already filthy skin skirt. She saw the fat which I had put aside to oil my hardax and, finished with the

cooked meat, speared fat with a stick and held it over
the fire. It sizzled and dripped, the droppings making
splashes of fire on the coals, and then she ate it.

"I am Mar," she said, wiping her mouth with the
back of her hand. "I will be your ——"

"I forbid you ever to use that word," I said sternly.

"It's a love word."

"It's a filth word."

"I obey," she said. "I will warm your back as you
sleep."

"No," I said. She stank. Not since skinning the dead
lion had I smelled such rot.

"I will sleep now and tomorrow you will return to
your village," I said. Not giving her a chance to answer, I rolled into my bed of leaves and grass. She sat
for a long time and then curled up on the ground near
the fire.

During the night she came and slept by my feet, her
hand touching my tough and blackened sole. Several
times I pulled my foot away, but each time she returned, the touch light and, somehow, comforting.

At dawn there was a chill in the air, and I left her
there sleeping while I hunted and shot a climber. He
was tough and stringy, but the meat, unlike the fatty
repast of the evening, was good. She ate more than her
share.

I set out at a fast pace. She kept stride with me,
which was more than any of my people could do. Her
legs were long and supple, like mine. Seeing that I did
not want to talk, she was silent. Beyond the low hill
there was a valley which stretched onward, with areas
of God's chaos strewn everywhere. I picked a likely
route. It was not, by any means, a straight line, since I
felt the warnings each time I neared an area of God's
chaos, and she questioned my wandering.

"You do not feel the warning?"

"What warning?"

"There," I said, pointing toward a rubbled area, stark and forbidding.

"There we find things," she said. "Building materials for our houses. Pretty things."

"There is death," I repeated. She looked at me strangely.

At midday we saw, coming to meet us, a small group. I considered moving to one side, but remembering the ease with which I'd handled two of the inbreeders, and knowing more curiosity than fear, I waited. The group consisted of a haired man, three small children and a woman far along toward giving life.

"Thank the gods," the man said, hurrying the last small distance to meet us. "A woman. My mate—"

"Is it time?" Mar asked.

"She has been feeling the pains since morning," he said.

Mar arranged the family's sleepskins in the meager shade of a runted tree, and the woman lay moaning as the convulsions came. I sat and watched. The man squatted on his heels. The children went off to explore the nearby countryside.

"There," I said, "to the east. Can you tell me of the country?"

The man shrugged. "What's to tell? The same."

"Have you been far?"

"Five days," he said. "We go to the coolness of the low hills."

"Are there dragons?"

"The dragon of the grass plain," he said. "Two days march, then go north past a range of wooded slopes to avoid his path."

"Tell me of him."

"A dragon is a dragon," he said. "He is old and has no teeth, but his eyes live, as he does."

Our talk was halted by a scream from the woman in labor, and I looked to see Mar lift a wet and repulsive bundle which, as she wiped it with grass, was a kicking and bawling baby, and then there was another. Eagerly, when Mar gave the signal that it was over, the man ran to the shade of the tree. I saw him halt in midstride. His wail was hoarse and painful. Curious, I went to look past him. One of the newly born was unlike anything human I'd ever seen. The skull had flowed down into what should have been the face, displacing one eye completely and moving the other low, where it glared out from beside a maw which replaced the nose, leaving only a gaping, raw, red hole. The mouth was small and lipless, and inside I could see tiny pointed teeth. The arms were flippers, as of a hardshell of the lakes, and the legs were shortened, with no feet at the end of rounded stubs.

With a hoarse cry, the father seized the thing and, holding it by its footless legs, dashed its horrible head against the tree. He tossed it aside and then raised the other baby to examine it. It was female, and it was active and well shaped.

"One out of one," the man said. "The gods are kind." He turned to me proudly. I was still sickened and shocked by his cruelty to the malformed young one.

"She will be called after your mate, who delivered her," he said. "And should it be your desire, she is yours as a gift, for, as you see, we have three already."

"Thank you," I said. "I have no time for a child."

"So be it," he said. "Perhaps you would like the oldest girl, there." He pointed. His oldest daughter was, perhaps, six summers. She was naked, save for a loincloth. "Of course," he said, "since she has survived the dangerous years, and is already good ——" he used the word which seemed to come to these people so easily—"I would have to have something. Say, that hardax you carry."

"Have you people no shame?" I exploded. I could stand the sight of him no longer. I turned and ran from the scene, heading east. I heard Mar running behind me. After a while I walked and she came to my side.

"You are different," she said. "Are you a holy man from the distant mountains?"

"I am of the mountains," I said.

"I should have known. God forgive me," she said. "Don't strike me dead because I tried to tempt you with my unworthy body, holy man."

I marched long and fast, and she stayed beside me uncomplainingly. When I found a suitable campsite I quickly built a couch of leaves and grass and, feeling sorry for her in her seeming helplessness, built one for her. Then, with a fire going, I found large fish in the stream, which were easily speared with my arrows. Mar watched with fascination.

"You are so wise."

"Children take fish in this fashion," I said.

"Let me try," she begged. I handed her the longbow. She fumbled with it. I put my arms around her to show her how to hold it, and the stench of her assaulted my nostrils.

"Gah," I said. "You smell long dead."

"If I were rich," she said, "I would have scents to make me smell sweet."

"There is a better and simpler way," I said. "There is the stream. It is bottomed with clean, white sand. Wash yourself."

"I obey," she said. She walked to the stream, cupped her hands, splashed water into her face and came, her face dripping, to smile at me. "Is that better?"

I could not believe that the inbreeders did not know the clean joy of a bath. "It would be better," I said, "if you removed your clothing, pounded it and rubbed it with stones to remove the stench and the biting insects, and rubbed yourself all over with sand."

She recoiled, shocked. "Holy father," she said, "are you mad?"

Well, it was her body, and as long as I didn't have

to smell it, so be it. I fed the two of us with roasted fish, which made a pleasant change of diet, and slept. I awoke with the stench of the dead lion in my nostrils and felt warmth at my back. She was cupped around me, making a pleasant little buzzing sound as she breathed. I pushed her away, and she groaned and came back to put one arm over me. It was overwhelming, the stench. I shook her awake.

"Get on the other side of the fire," I said, "in your own bed."

She went, weeping. "What kind of man are you to deny a woman the pleasure of the warmth of your body on a chill night?" she protested.

"When you cease to smell like a dead lion I will warm you," I said.

"You are cruel and horrible and totally uncivilized," she said, turning her back and burrowing down into her couch.

I? Uncivilized? I leaped to my feet. I dragged her by the arm from her couch. "I will show you civilization," I said, pulling her toward the stream. She seemed to realize my intentions and began to scream and fight. I found myself with an armful of woman and had to use all my strength to subdue her without hurting her. When I had her bundled into my arms she was still kicking and wailing, and then I was at the stream. I threw her bodily into it. She landed with a great splash and came to the surface, spitting water. There was a full moon, and I could see the beams of it reflecting, shattered by her splash. She screamed and started flailing the water and went under.

The fool was going to drown in water which came only to her waist. I waded in, pulled her by the hair to her feet and got a few scratches as she tried to climb my body as if I were a tree. When at last I had her calmed, she stood there, my arms around her, shivering and weeping.

"You will kill me," she said.

"I am only going to wash you," I said. And, so saying, I began to take the clothing off her. She seemed resigned at first, letting me denude her. I had a shock when her breasts were bared, for, slim as she was, she had beautiful, large, full woman's breasts.

"Now," I said, "kneel, bring sand from the bottom, rub it over your skin. I will wash your clothing."

"You are going to kill me," she said.

"Oh, gods," I said. I took handfuls of sand, and as she stood there, weeping, I scrubbed her, feeling a strangeness in my body as my hands covered the roundness of her body, the hips, the hard back and soft rump, the full legs. To do the job right I washed thoroughly between her legs, and when I was doing that she ceased her sobbing for a moment and, in the moonlight, looked at me with her eyes half closed.

I scrubbed her until her skin was red and then washed her long hair repeatedly until, by sniffing her in various places, I detected only the fresh and natural scents of a clean body.

I led her from the stream. "Go to the fire," I said. "Warm yourself. I will wash your skins." She went. I beat her clothing with stones and rubbed it with stones and rinsed it repeatedly, and finally, after a long time, it was reasonably clean, but with a faint lingering aroma. Then I went to the fire. She was in her own couch, curled into a ball. I put her clothing onto a bush to dry and removed my own wet hides. I rubbed the water from my skin, shivering with the chill.

In my couch I pulled leaves to cover me. She had her back turned. If that was the way she wanted it, so be it. I slept. I awoke, feeling only a short passage of time, to feel her soft warmth at my back. It was pleasant, and there was only the fresh scent of cleanliness. I could tell by her breathing that she was not asleep.

"Much better," I said. "Now we can give each other warmth."

"I will die of the chill," she said.

She was shivering. Feeling slightly guilty, I turned and put my arms around her to give her my warmth. Her softness was disturbing. There was no sin in my actions. Nor was there sin when, with a sigh, she lifted her head and placed her lips on mine. All premen and prewomen may play so. And it was pleasant. Her lips full, soft. Her hands clasped my back and gave little spots of warmth. I let my hands know her back and her soft rump and, although she was not protected with a loincloth, carefully avoided the forbidden spot. I had done as much many times with Yuree, and the memory of it was white-hot pain. I ceased my activity. She did not. I lay as if made of stone, and her hands went to my manhood, and it grew, and then she was atop me, her weight sweet, and I was still thinking of Yuree when I felt myself touch the forbidden and her hand guiding me.

"It is sin," I gasped, trying to push her away. She clung and engulfed me, and I was weak, knowing feelings which I had never known.

And what was one more sin on the head of a killer of his own people?

We slept little as she taught me.

"You are not—were not—prewoman," I said, during a lull.

"What?"

"Oh, yes," I said, "you said you had a mate, who died or was killed."

"Yes. But none like you," she whispered.

"Now you will be with child," I said.

"No. I am barren."

"That is sad," I said. Barrenness was not unknown to my people.

"I would have taken the little girl," she said.

"Perhaps you are not barren, after all."

She laughed. "I have tried many times with many mates."

I was shocked. I rolled away and gave her my back.

"Did I say something wrong?" she asked.

"Many mates?" I asked, feeling jealousy.

"Oh, as many as my fingers, no more."

"Shame," I said.

"You speak of shame and you a holy man?"

"I am not a holy man."

"Then you are mad."

"Perhaps," I said. I was silent. At last, I went to sleep. When I awoke she was cooking the fish which I had suspended in a tree out of the reach of small animals. I ate. I resolved not to repeat my sin with her, but my resolution failed after we had eaten and she came to me.

We spent half a moon there, near the stream, and in that time I taught her and she taught me. She learned, finally, that fatal chills do not come from wetting the body all over, and, indeed, before we left she had begun to swim in a frantic, flailing, half-sinking sort of way.

I had utilized the time to kill climbers, tan their hides, and fashion her a garment, using the few strands of dragon's veins which I had to hold it together. She looked charming in her reddish skirt which rose to cover her breasts and hang by one strap across a tanned shoulder, and I found myself forgetting, for long periods at a time, that I was Eban the Killer of his People and that I had lost happiness when the killbird struck the father of my intended pairmate. I could even forget, for a while, when Mar was in my arms, that she had known other men, as many as her fingers.

Mar was, as best she could account, the number of summers counted by the fingers of two hands and the toes of one foot. She had no numbers, as I did. I told her that was fifteen, and she said, "Yes, two hands and one foot."

It was a signal of coming winter which broke into my idleness, my happiness there in that grove of stunted trees beside the stream where big fish swam. "We must go," I said.

"We will go back to my village, there to spend the winter in my house," she said.

"We will not," I said. "We will go to the south and the east."

"There be dragons," she said fearfully.

"It is you who followed me, knowing my intentions."

"I did not know you were mad and would go to the east forever."

"Perhaps not forever," I said. Why was I driven? I had Mar. Although game was not as plentiful, and was small and stringy, there was game in those flatlands. I could have built a hut, a cave, something. But there were those moments when I remembered and knew that to the east was my salvation, the deliverance of Eban the Killer of His People. There was death, and an honorable death at God's will and not from my own hand.

There was Mar, however. Had I the right to risk her life?

"Mar," I said, "there will be danger. When there is, I will warn you and you will retreat. If I am killed, you will go back to your people."

"It is far," she said. "I would not be able to find them. I would starve."

"Follow the setting sun," I said. "And I will prepare food for you, food which will last."

I dried meat in the sun, carrying it as we journeyed uneventfully toward the south and east, staying just ahead of winter. We encountered few of the inbreeders, avoiding them as I avoided the more and more numerous areas of God's chaos.

At night the winter stars were the same as those of my mountains. And many times, as I lay awake, I saw God's messengers, stars larger than the rest, high, swiftly moving, traveling from flat horizon to flat horizon. I did not know what I sought. I had nothing for which to live, save Mar. And she would not mourn me, for she had known men, as many as the fingers of two hands.

4

I fully expected to be dead. Now the time of long nights was nearing. From the notches I'd made on the handle of my hardax I knew that the new moon was the first moon of the winter and that in the mountains there would now be snow, the animals entering into the long harshness of shortage, the deer growing poorer as the days passed, the great bear sleeping, but in this strange land the winter's breath was merely a frost, a thin layer of white which melted and faded with the rise of the sun, and although the nights were cold, the days were warm. Once I tried to estimate, at the end of a purposeful but not strenuous day's walk, the distance we had covered in arrow flights. The numbers grew until they were beyond my comprehension, and the total distance between me and my home and my people was of such a vastness!

And I was not dead. We heard talk of dragons, and we saw, in the few people we encountered—so far south and east were we now, at the start of winter, that we went a full moon without seeing a trace of man, and then only in the form of a corpse left lying beside a woodland—the signs of death. Few wandered so far. One day we saw a new kind of bird, white, flying low and crying out with a raucous screech. The air smelled different, damp, humid, even on the chill days of early winter.

Mar could not understand, nor, in confidence, could I, the urge which kept me going. Past death now, I think, looking back, that it was pride, or perhaps curiosity. Could it all be such a sameness? The flat, slightly rolling ground, the stunted trees, the occasional streams, the vast and sprawling heaps of God's chaos? It was far more dangerous in the mountains, with lions, bears and dragons. Dragons in the east? Ha. We had *heard* of dragons, for example the dragon of the grassy plain, but we had seen none. I concluded that the only danger in the east was to people like Mar, who, I had concluded, did not have the gift of the warning, could not feel the spirits of the dead, perhaps the dead giants, calling out from the chaos of God to tell of death. Someday, I thought, I would return and tell the people of the mountains, the only true men, that there was no danger in the far hills nor beyond. They would not believe me, of course, for from childhood man was taught that death lay there, and had been taught so for so many generations that it was a part of our legacy.

Perhaps I still sinned in my pride, thinking that someday I would return and tell strange tales and, perhaps, enrich the knowledge of my people. At any rate, I continued on more east now than south, and the countryside changed from rolling hills to a flat plain with only mild undulations, scanty vegetation, and even scantier game, consisting mostly of little rodents and hares. The soil was sandy and coarse and poor, and now and then, where there was chaos, the surface could be seen from a distance to have a sheen, as if made of sand-colored ice. But the areas of warning, the heaps of God's chaos, were more scattered.

We encountered a large river and followed it. There were trees along the stream, and the water was drinkable, if muddy. I began to wonder if that river would lead to the fabled field of large waters, the unending lake, or if that was merely some myth out of our past.

We encountered swamps along the river, sometimes pushing through them, sometimes skirting them. In the swamps were wondrous creatures, snakes which did not flee, as did the harmless snakes of the mountains, but stayed to fight and poison their prey with their fangs, larger reptiles with huge scales, turtles, and a delicious large variety of frog, the legs of which made feasts equaled only by the meat of the fanged serpents.

To build up enough frog's legs for a meal, we entered one swamp, waded, found high ground, killed snakes and frogs until, seeing a rise ahead, we carried our booty out through thick woods to step without much forethought into an open field grown with a tall form of grass. I froze instantly and then went into action, thrusting Mar back into the trees. There, within arrow flight, was the old and bloody head of a dragon. Thank God he had been sleeping.

We circled and came out of the swamp in another area, carefully this time, and, gods of man, there were dragons everywhere, ancient, their blood coloring their hides, their heads motionless but deadly. All the dragons of the world seemed to be congregated in that field. I could not help but stay to stare and think of all the riches inside those beasts, and for a long time I counted, reaching three hundred before I forgot which dragons I had counted. And all the time none of them moved. I began to notice things. The nearest dragon sagged on his feet, his belly on the rankly grown ground, a gaping hole in his side. He looked as dead as the dragon I'd killed.

"Here, dragon," I called, standing for a moment, exposed. I leaped back, but there was no hail of teeth, no flash of deadly eyes.

While Mar cowered among the trees, I stepped out into the weed-grown field and dared them, all of the tens of dragons which I could see. None moved. All were holed, battered, dead on their feet. I danced and sang. I called out to them, always ready to leap for safety. Nothing. Leaving Mar in shelter, I crawled toward the nearest dragon. I gained the shelter of its tough-skinned hide, below the holes which spat teeth and the glaring eyes, most of which were shattered. He was dead. Very dead. I looked into the hole in his side, and there, exposed, were his guts. I made use of them, jerking them out one at a time, and, sitting there calling for Mar to join me, I wove a necklace for her. She refused to come. She was frightened. I kept calling, and finally she edged out, broke into a run and fell heavily down beside me, winded. I put the necklace of dragon's guts around her neck. She threw it off and shuddered.

That woman. Throwing away what any civilized woman would have done most anything to own. I retrieved it. "Look," I said, "I know you're uneducated, but this is silly."

"I don't want dirty dragon's guts on me," she said.

"Are they not pretty?"

"Well, yes, in a sort of way," she admitted.

"Among my people they are treasured and worn by only the bravest of the brave, those who have slain dragons."

"Ugg," Mar said, as I put the necklace back around her neck.

Slowly, cautiously, I began to explore the field of the dead dragons. Soon I became confident. They were all dead. I moved freely from one to the other. All were damaged. One was split wide open. I explored. There were plenty of veins for the taking, so I stocked up and then found smaller pieces of broken skin suitable for arrow heads. A clear piece of something, dragon's bone, maybe, was so sharp I kept it. It would be great for scraping skins. It was rounded on one edge, about a finger's joint thick, and sheared into a sharp edge which ran across the curve of it. I could look through it and see things on the other side, but they were distorted and twisted, curved and funny.

Never had I seen such a treasure as that field of dragons.

"It must be," I said, "where all dragons come to die."

"Then let us leave, before one comes which is not quite dead," Mar said.

The animals of the fields had made nests in some of the dragons. It was good hunting. We slept there, in that graveyard of terrible beasts, Mar clinging closely to me. And then, since I, too, felt the hovering spirits of the dead during the dark and chill night, we put it behind us and crossed a huge dragon's track. We had seen many tracks, all weed-grown, broken, rotting, but this was the largest. I thought that mates, two dragons, had beaten it down, for there were twin paths which ran side by side, up rise and down slope into the distance. There were no fresh tracks. Since the dragon path went east, I elected to follow it. I learned more about dragons, deciding that they were wondrous beasts, able to use white bones to span streams, their paths suspended high above the water below.

We came, after two days of following the dragon's path, to an area of God's chaos and had to leave it with the warning of the spirits tickling my belly. I killed a small deer and dressed it, but upon doing the work which, at home, was done by the house of Yorerie the Butcher, I felt the warning tingle, very faint, and narrowed down its source to the bones of the stunted deer. It was my first experience of the kind, and it created wonder in my mind. That night, as an experiment, while cuddled close to Mar, I opened myself, making my skin its most sensitive, and pressed tightly against her. In the areas where her bones were near the surface, as on the wrists and ankles, I could feel it, ever so faint, the small tingle of warning. It caused me much alarm. I reasoned, however, that any contamination would have already been accomplished, and she, herself, seemed healthy enough. Indeed, in spite of our constant travel, with my provisions she had gained weight and was now more womanly, rounder, softer than ever. It was a puzzle, however.

The next day proved to be one of the more eventful ones of my life. We set out eastward early, but skirting the large chaos on the dragon's path. We saw ahead a woodland which seemed out of keeping with the stunted and twisted trees of the region, and I made for it, thinking to kill an untainted deer, or at the least to add another deerskin—I had saved the other one, since there was no spirit warning in the hide—to our stock of bedclothes and apparel. It was a beautiful wood, with huge trees bearing the nuts eaten by the climber, trees which had trunks so huge that a hidehouse could have been hidden behind without showing. The ground was soft with the fall of seasons and seasons of leaves. There was game sign. I did kill another small deer, but it too had the warning spirit in its bones, so we ate none, much to Mar's disgust. Now, indeed, the rodents and hares had the spirit in their bones, and our diet was narrowed to nuts and to the climbers, tough and stringy as they were. I experimented, and the root things which grew in the ground gave me the tiny tingle of warning. I was concerned, but there was no tingle as long as I did not come near a buried root thing which had been unearthed, or if I did not break into the bones of the animals from which came the warning.

"Look," I said, "here we are not freaks, for even the trees have hair."

It was so. They were festooned with gray hair. It gave the woods a sober, secluded and lonely look. It was not true hair, of course, for upon examination it proved to be a tasteless thing of vegetable material, not strong enough to use for any purpose.

"I like it here," Mar said. "And I am tired of travel. Let us build a house and stay."

"We will explore the woodland first," I said, leading her deeper into the darkness of the huge trees. I was teaching her to use the hunter's stalk, to walk silently. We crept ahead as quietly as two ghosts, and I saw up ahead something which caused my blood to soar and send me for cover, pulling Mar behind me. It was the glint of dragonskin. There was no mistaking it.

Leaving Mar in safety, I crept from tree to tree until I could see the nature of the thing. It was a strangeness, webbed in regular patterns like a spider's nest. Three times my height, it extended to right and left. I threw a stick at it from a safe distance, and there was nothing. I threw another and hit it and there was a sound, but no spitting of teeth nor flash of deadly eyes. And then I began to notice that beyond the web was a greenness which was unlike anything I'd ever seen. I crept closer. There was an expanse of grass, but growing low and evenly. In patterns in the grassy field there were bushes, some with large white flowers which were totally out of place in the winter. After testing each step carefully, I stood beside the dragonskin web. I touched it with my hardax. Nothing. I tried to cut it. My hardax bounced off.

There was no danger. I went back for Mar and showed her the wonders. Nothing would do but for her to have some of the white flowers. I touched the web. It was cold and hard, dragonskin. I tried to climb it. By putting my toes in the mesh I could. I gained the top and reached down for Mar and lifted her. Then we dropped to the other side, though with some painful cuts caused by sharp edges on the top of the web. The grass was soft and pliant under our feet. We walked toward the nearest bush with white flowers, I on the alert, listening for any sound, sensitive to spirits. Mar ran ahead and was plucking the white flowers. They smelled sweet.

"It's beautiful here," she said.

"The grass is sick," I said. "It grows thickly but directly atop the dirt." I didn't like it.

"Still, you feel none of what you call the warning," she said.

"No."

But there was a strangeness. And then I knew, for I heard it, a whining creak, not as loud as the wail of my slain dragon, but of the same texture of sound. I searched for a place to hide. There was only the bushes. They would offer no protection against a hail of dragon's teeth. Suddenly I understood. There were dragons and there were dragons, and this was a type of dragon which beat down grass for his path instead of dirt and stone.

I pulled Mar into the bushes, and we crouched as the sound drew near, coming toward us from clumps of bushes and trees which hid the view. I held my breath. He came around a clump of bushes. He was a small dragon, about as wide at the ground as I was tall, but shorter than my body. He would come, I estimated, to my waist. He moved slowly, and he was eating, cropping the grass and spitting out the unused portions behind him. He made creaking and humming sounds. He came directly toward us. I would have to fight if he sensed us, hidden behind the useless bushes. He had only one eye, directly in front, and his head seemed to be a part of his body, unable to turn as had the head of my dragon. That gave me hope. I might be able to come up on his blind side.

I readied myself. The dragon came directly toward us, and I tensed, ready to leap and die trying to blind him with an ax stroke to his one vulnerable spot, the eye. But just before he entered the bushes, seemingly bent on seeking us out, he turned and went away. Dragons, thank the gods of man, had no noses.

What? Was I a little disappointed? Perhaps. I had traveled far and I had seen the dying place of the huge dragons, and this tiny dragon who had come so close seemed to me to be easy prey. In my pride, I leaped up, ran after the fleeing dragon lightly, leaped upon his back and with one crushing blow smashed his sensitive eye. He stopped. There was a dying hum from inside. He was dead.

"Come and see," I called. Mar came fearfully. I turned the dragon onto his back. He had teeth with sharp edges, huge teeth, stained by the grass which was his food. I beat upon him a bit with my ax, but did not want to ruin the edge, so we left him upturned, vanquished.

"How can you be so brave?" Mar asked admiringly. My chest swelled.

"Smaller dragons slain to order," I said lightly.

I didn't feel so brave when, walking along in the direction from which the dragon had come, there was a sudden hiss of sound and it rained from the ground. Water, rain, flew upward, wetting us. Mar screamed. I was frozen for only an instant. It was only rain, and if it came from the ground, what else could we expect in this strange land? Mar tried to run, and I grabbed her arm. We walked through the rain and rounded a clump of bushes, and there, face to face, we came upon another of the grass-eating dragons. He had us, eye on. I yelled and rushed, expecting an instant hail of spat teeth or a flash of burning eye, but the creature, instead of spitting or blazing, merely continued toward me, making a creak and a hum and I killed him head on, smashing his eye with one blow.

A baby dragon? There was no blood, no signs of age. Was that why I lived? I examined him carefully, much more carefully than the first. There were no holes for spitting teeth. Did they develop with age? Had we found the birthplace of dragons? Did dragons breed, after all?

But I was soon to have other worries, for Mar was tugging on my arm and pointing. "Look, oh, look."

I looked. Through the bushes, the trees, there was a gleam of pure white. My blood froze. So huge a dragon. The mother of all dragons. She would spit. She would burn. And I saw, reflected in the light of the afternoon sun, a dozen eyes of a hugeness which made me forget all my bravery. I ran. I ran and left Mar to follow. And I stopped running only when I reached the web. I was trying to climb it when she caught up. "Help me, help me," she cried. We clambered over the web at the expense of more cuts.

It was a full day before I had the courage to go back to the web. We walked along it. It was huge. We reached a place where it changed. I checked for danger and we started to walk past a different kind of web and suddenly there was movement. We ran to the trees and watched as the section of the web which had swung back slowly closed the gap left. I went back, stood there again, moved about. The web sprang open.

"It's alive," Mar gasped.

No teeth holes. No eyes. It was more and more curious.

"We will go in," I said.

"Oh, God, no."

"We went in before."

"There's the huge dragon."

"We will watch for him."

We went in. A different kind of dragon's path awaited us, surfaced with small, loose stones. There were no dragon's tracks on it, however, and, emboldened, I led the trembling Mar onward along an avenue of huge trees, until, once again, we caught the gleam of white through the trees. I left her and went forward, tree by tree. I could not get an overall view of the dragon, it was that huge. But I got closer and closer without incident. When I was near, I could see that the dragon extended upward, had a covering of long, regular pieces of bone which looked like stone, had eyes which were square-cornered, some tall, some short, eyes which reflected light. It was a puzzle. The dragon seemed to sit on a wall of stones of regular shape, as if anchored permanently. Experimentally, I showed myself. Nothing happened. I threw a small stone and it clanked off the side of the dragon. Still nothing. I threw a larger stone, aiming for an eye. The stone shattered the eye, and I waited for the dragon to roar, but there was only silence until I saw movement from a part of the huge thing and a plate opened and out came a small dragon which carried an eye in the form of a large sheet of the type of bone which I'd scavenged from the dead dragon in the field of the dead. I could see through it. I watched in amazement as the little dragon sprouted legs, grew upward, carrying the eye, and, after clearing the socket of shatters, replaced the eye. I shattered another, and the same thing happened, and as the little dragon worked I stood in the clear. I went unnoticed. I edged closer and as the dragon finished his job and came down, folding his legs inside his body, I leaped forward and smashed his eye with my ax. He died, the hum fading slowly.

Feeling very brave and not a little foolhardy, I explored, being so close to the huge thing without being dead. The skin was not dragonskin, but seemed to be wood—I made little dents with my ax and had to leap quickly as a small dragon came out and sprayed the white stuff which covered the wood over the dents I'd made. You see, by that time, not being stupid, I had figured out that these small dragons had no teeth and that their eyes were not deadly. To prove it, I walked directly in front of the little dragon which spit out the white stuff and he ignored me. I smashed his eye and he died.

So, I thought, what treasures are here, unprotected? I went back for Mar. She was frightened of coming with me but more frightened of staying. We approached the huge white thing and found stone, formed as layers which led upward like the exposed rocks of a hillside, only neat and in lines. We stood on the thing, under a part of it, nervous, admittedly, but more and more confident that there was no danger. As we came close to the side of it a plate opened. It took a little while to decide to go into the thing's maw. But go we did, and there was softness underfoot. In a place like a cave, the plate closed behind us. I panicked. I ran and started to cut my way out, but the plate swung open. I experimented. Any time I wanted to go out, the plate opened. We moved forward. Mar and I both still dripped water from being wet in the rain which came from the ground, and it was staining the strange, soft thing under our feet. I heard a sound, saw a small plate open in the wall and a tiny dragon came purring out. I raised my ax. The dragon went to the water stains, made a purring sound, and the water stains disappeared, eaten. The dragon moved toward us and then halted, waiting for us to move. We moved, and he ate the water stains. I felt a little nervous, even if he did seem harmless, so I smashed his little eye. He died. Immediately another plate opened and another dragon of a different sort came out, picked up the dead one, and went away.

"You should have killed him, too," Mar said. "He'll tell others that we're here."

I said nothing. I looked around. There were plates all around the cavelike place. I stood in front of one, and it opened. Another cave, much larger, was before us. I stepped in. The sun came out suddenly in the form of a glow which lit the cave brightly, and I looked wildly around for a dragon, finding none.

I suppose when you feel fear so often, you grow immune. Heart pounding with the suddenness of the light, I waited. I looked around. There were things, huge things, colored and soft-looking. They reminded me of chairs and couches. But they were huge. And my blood went cold.

"There were giants in those days," the old storytellers said.

"Gods of man," I said. "We are in the house of the giants."

"Eban, let's go," Mar said, clinging to my arm.

"The treasures here!" I said. I walked to one of the eyes, saw outside the close-growing grass, the bushes with white flowers. The eye was partially covered with a sort of skin which went to the top, and, when touched, was wondrously soft and thin, unlike any skin, however well scraped, I'd ever seen. Thinner than the membrane of guts, white, delicate. I ripped down a huge piece of it. I draped it around Mar's shoulders.

"Gods, it's so beautiful," she said.

"Treasures," I said. "We are so rich."

"And if the giants come home?"

"The giants are dead. They are as old as the dragons."

I sat in a chair thing. It dwarfed me. It was soft and yielding. Mar, seeing my bravery, tried a couch thing, and ended up bouncing on it, yelling happily as she sprang into the air. I tried another. I heard a small click and leaped, but not soon enough. A plate opened on the wall and an eye of big and white horror glared at us, and there was a sizzling, grinding sound and white flashes in the eye and then a sound like rushing water and flickers of light in the eye, but we were looking back on it from the first cave. When nothing happened and the eye went out and the plate closed we went back, but soon tired of the couch things and the chair things.

Another cave had a bottom of stone and was nearly empty, but when we walked in and stepped onto the cold stone a hideous sound broke out and continued as long as we stood on the stone. It was a sound which I cannot describe, consisting of many things, some like the screech of a dragon, some soft like the wind in the trees, and under it all a rhythm which reminded me of old Seer of Things Unseen beating on her treedrum. But all in all it was a grating noise, and we soon tired of it to find, at the end of a long cave, the most wondrous cave of all, a cave of multiple plates which opened at a touch, revealing incredible things. There were frail cups, not nearly as sturdy as the cups which my family made of fire-hardened clay, and huge plates, and other things, some of dragonskin, and the most amazing thing, a whole collection of skinning knives so wonderfully wrought that there was no blood and so sharp that I could have scraped away my hair. I chose several, thrusting them into my loincloth, and gave Mar two to carry for me. I could, with those knives, skin the largest bear with no effort at all.

We climbed a cave with steps and found couches and things we knew not, huge bowls on the floor of some small caves, for example. We liked the lower caves better, and satisfied that we were alone, decided to spend the night. It was not cold inside the caves, as it was growing with the lateness of the evening outside, but a hunter has his fire. I cast around for a place and decided that the best place, with the clearest field of vision, was the room with the stone floor, if only I could stop the dreadful sounds which sprang out of the walls when we entered. I solved the problem by following my ears to find the places where the sounds originated and stopped them with several blows of the hardax. Then it was quiet. I used the ax to break up some chair things—having to take time out to kill at least half a dozen small dragons who seemed to be intent on stealing my firewood—and started my fire on the stone floor in the center of the room. It was a cheerful sight, even though the magic sunlight lit the room well. The smoke rose and began to collect, and I decided that we needed a vent, so I knocked out a couple of eyes with my stone ax, and soon there was a dragon outside putting the eyes back into place, and no sooner did I knock one out than he was there putting it back. By then the cave was filling with smoke. Mar was coughing. And then she screamed, as it began to rain, and the rain was not mere water, but a smelly, sticky whiteness which cascaded down from the roof of the cave. Our fire was quickly out and we were covered by the stuff, and there were dragons everywhere cleaning up the remains of our fire and the white stuff.

"Enough," I said, smashing dragon's eyes right and left. "We leave this place and seek sensible shelter in the woods."

"Yes, yes," Mar said.

Just to give the dragons something to do, I smashed a few eyes from the outside and threw a burning brand into two or three of them to watch the white rain fall. Then it was night. We went into the woodlands and built a small lean-to and a roaring fire, and Mar was, happily, my ———. I had come to accept the word.

5

Now winter found us. Ice froze in still waters in the swamps. The small animals hid in their burrows, the climbers in their nests, and I was thankful for the sun-dried meat which I carried in my pack, fashioned of part of a deerskin. There were nuts to eat and a small black berry which I observed to be clean, since the birds liked it and it gave, unlike most of the vegetation, no warning of spirits. We ate climbers until I longed for a huge and juicy deer haunch roasted on a spit over a fire of cinders from our long-burning hardwoods of the mountains.

We moved eastward from the grove wherein sat the cave of the giants with its toothless small dragons. Mar begged to be allowed to stop, to build a mud-and-grass hut where we could warm ourselves with a fire vented by a hole in the center of the roof and by lying together in our couch. However, the cold was minor compared to the deadly and snow-deep winters of the mountains, so I pushed on, finding shelter as we might; for example, in the lee of a huge fallen tree with a makeshift lean-to of branches over us. I had it in my mind to find the legendary field of endless waters, and I felt that it must be near, for there was a smell to the air.

I was frustrated in my desire to continue eastward by increasing spirit warning, and we spent long and aimless days wandering to the south, trying to find a gap in the solid wall of warning which lay to the east.

The reptiles and frogs were sleeping, hidden from the cold. I found that fat birds of the water were clean and, although tasting somewhat fishy, were nourishing and quite easily taken by arrow, since they had no fear of man.

Most of the woodlands were of an evergreen tree, tall and straight, with needles similar to the evergreens of our mountains. The climbers ate of the burred seeds, as did we, but found them to be rather tasteless.

The warning tingle in my belly was, at times, very strong and caused retreat, so that for the early winter months our course angled east and back and ever southward. The days began to vary, some of them pleasantly warm, some chill as the wind shifted into the north, but gradually it warmed and then there were new green shoots growing and the animals were partaking in the new-year ritual of mating and food was more plentiful.

The new year was well established when I decided that it was not my lot to see the field of endless waters. Everywhere to the east was a solid wall of warning. The spirits, it seemed, had reason to guard the endless waters from the eyes of man, or at least of man with the sense to heed the warnings.

I make mention of one incident, which decided me to alter my plans. Finding a gap in the wall of warning spirits, we ventured eastward into woodlands and found climbers plentiful and, testing with a stunted deer, the same warning in the very bones of the beast. It was when we were camped for the night beside a pleasant lake. The fire had been allowed to burn down, and I heard, as I fell into sleep, the stealthy movements of an animal. I alerted myself and reached for my longbow and saw, reflecting the dying gleam of the fire, a pair of eyes at a height from the ground which caused me concern. Quickly I replenished the fire, and the eyes disappeared, but I had little sleep that night.

In the morning I saw tracks, much like the tracks of

a lion, only different. There were claw marks on each pad, whereas a lion walks with his claws withdrawn. I continued eastward with some caution. I saw hints of movement in the trees around us. There was more than one animal there, and I knew the feeling of being stalked, as I'd known it when the lion of the mountains sought me for his meal.

As usual, the warnings came and we had to retreat, through the same stretch of woodlands, and that night there were two, three, four sets of eyes around our campfire. I wanted to get to the bottom of it. I picked my chance, aimed a hand below the gleaming set of eyes with my straightest arrow and heard an eerie yowl as the arrow went home. There was a threshing sound and then silence, and then a series of mournful hoots, sounding almost human. It was too much for me. I built the fire to its greatest with armloads of dry branches gathered before darkness, and the light showed a heap on the ground and eyes in the darkness behind it. I set a branch blazing and walked nervously to take a look at my kill.

I cried out in fear when I saw it. The thing lay on its back. Its pink eyes were open, and blood ran down my arrow shaft where it had lodged in the throat below a face out of a nightmare, a face which was near human but distorted into wide-eyed horror, with fangs which extended over huge, thick lips and a mouth large enough to cover the lower face. The body was all haired and the arms were long and there were three fingers on each hand and the feet were huge and haired and vaguely human but clubbed into a shortness which made them look like lion's paws.

The thing was almost as tall as I. Its vaguely human features and shape told me that it might walk upright, and the height of the glowing eyes, when they had first caught the firelight, confirmed it. Shaken, I went to my fire and tended it all night, and in the early hours of the morning there was a scuffling and hooting moans which caused the hair of my neck to rise. At the sound of growling, I threw a brand to see, in the brief flare of light, a sight which chilled my blood. A half dozen of the things were tearing and ripping at the body of their dead fellow, fangs chewing, with blood dripping down their hair-covered faces. Sickened, I yelled and charged them with a burning brand, and one of them stood his ground, indeed, made threatening moves toward me, his huge mouth open to show the fearsome teeth, his growl low and feral. I sent an arrow into his midsection and he fell, but crawled away to moan and scream until I heard a flurry of movement and knew that he, too, was furnishing a meal for his kind. The eating sounds, accompanied by sounds of struggle and occasional hoots, as if of pain, continued until light, and I decided that it was wise for us to leave those woods. We seemed to be in the clear when, without warning, one of the manlike beasts leaped a tree to send Mar sprawling to the ground, and four others charged us from the undergrowth. I used one of the dragonskin skinning knives to kill the beast which was trying to reach Mar's jugular with his fanged teeth and rose quickly to swing my hardax at the first of the oncoming attackers. He fell, his head almost severed, and I struck the arm of a second such a blow that he was no longer interested in combat. But I went down under the remaining two, using my knife to disembowel one, feeling the sharp teeth of the other on my shoulder, buried under the weight of the dying one and the other, who was fighting to bite my neck. I was in a bad way for a moment, and then the attacker was jerked, went limp and began, still atop me, to kick out his life. I scrambled out from under the reeking mass of horror and saw Mar, breathing hard, crouched over us, one of her knives bloody.

"Well done," I said.

"Are you hurt?"

"Only a scratch," I said, squeezing the wounds on

my shoulder to force them to purify themselves with free bleeding. Later I would cover them with a leaf poultice.

I took time to examine the fallen ones and was struck by the nearness to human form. It was as if some cruel god had taken a man and done his best to deform him, make him a horrible imitation of man. But there were hoots from the forest, and I led Mar away as quickly as I could until, gaining fairly open ground, we left the dark and terrible things behind us.

I was left without a purpose. What little purpose I had had was involved with seeing the fabled field of endless water, and, prevented from seeking that goal by the continuous belt of warning which cut me off from traveling east, I made a semipermanent camp and watched the days grow longer. This pleased Mar. She blossomed. She found clay and formed cups, plates, bowls, fired them in the campfire. She became very domestic.

But as the weather warmed and it was impossible to move without breaking out in sweat, and, worse, the flying biters came in clouds, I tired of those hot, humid lowlands and, to Mar's sadness, made movement to the west. I longed for the coolness of my native mountains. However, it was impossible for me to return to my own home. I had been the bringer of death to half of my family. And to come, bringing with me one of the sick women of the low ridges, would be the ultimate insult and would, most probably, invite trial before the elders of the family, with the ultimate punishment being what I was already suffering, banishment.

However, the mountains were long and large and there was the talk I had listened to in my youth, of the hills extending far to the southward to diminish into pleasant rolling lands.

We followed the sun westward, through a broiling summer which left us weak and exhausted at the end of the day. But the farther we went westward the more plentiful became the game, the clearer became the streams. Since our march eastward had been less purposeful, we made better time on the westward march, for I did not deviate, except to avoid the areas of God's chaos. One moon after the longest days of summer we saw on a clear day a band of blue to the west which looked like low storm clouds, but as the days passed, it grew, until, my heart leaping with joy, I knew that there were the mountains.

Now we encountered men, the same sick, weak, starving men of Mar's country, not to be trusted. My wanderings and the passing time had added weight to my body, and, with my face hair full, my skull hair hanging to my shoulders, I was, no doubt, a fearsome sight, and my efforts to avoid the inbreeders of the low slopes were not contested by them. Nevertheless, I kept one eye open as I slept and two or three times had to growl warning, once to fire an arrow, to drive off prowlers.

At last we reached the low hills leading upward to the mountains, which, as I had expected, did not look as high as the mountains of my home.

On a night of nights, I came to our camp with a huge and healthy deer and we spent three days in that camp feasting and preparing meat to dry in the sun. I taught Mar how to chew the hide to make it soft and pliant. Now she would be properly dressed for winter in our own—in my own—type of country, for I had had enough of wandering and would, I had decided, make my home in some secluded place in the mountains.

Laden with drying meat, my stock of dragon's veins, the beautiful and deadly skinning knives from the cave of the giants, my hardax, our sleepskins and the new deerskin, we climbed the low hills, and in my eagerness to find the coolness of the heights we walked into the range of an old dragon, a dragon of the hills.

It came without warning. I topped a ridge, Mar at

my side, her legs strong, long, keeping pace with me, and I saw the bloodstained, ancient body of the dragon even as his head jerked and there came the creaking, warning scream of his anger and then a burst of sound and things like bees buzzing as his teeth flew around us. I yelled and fell back, dragging Mar with me behind the dome of the ridge. She lay limply. I pulled her farther down the slope, thinking she was merely frightened and tired. She was unmoving, and there was a great flow of blood into her black hair, and I felt my heart hurt. The dragon had spat teeth into her head.

Oh, gods of man, I prayed. I rolled her onto her back. Her eyes were closed. She was, I felt, dead. The lion had been spat in the head by my dragon, and he was ever so much stronger than my poor Mar. So I mourned for a moment and then, in my agony, saw her chest moving. She was breathing. I parted her hair and saw that the tooth had not broken her skull, but merely chewed along it, taking a small groove of flesh and hair. I carried her to water, a stream which we had passed not long before, and bathed her head in the coolness, finally stopping the flow of blood. But still she slept.

"Mar, Mar, without you I am again alone," I told her.

She heard not.

Through a long and sad afternoon and through the night I sat beside her. She opened her eyes with the morning sun and looked at me as if she did not see me and went back to sleep, but I now had hope.

It is said that out of chaos comes good, but it is not always true. What good comes from God's chaos of the eastern flats? Sickness and death. But, true, in the mountains the chaos of the fires from God's anger from the skies clears the underbrush and leaves growing room for new and tender things.

Out of God's blow to Mar came good in the long run, I suppose, for it taught me that I needed her. To that point I had considered her merely a ———, that dirty word of her people. And a companion. Someone with whom to talk. Now, thinking that she was dead, a hurting in my chest, tears on my face, all the pain, told me that she had become more, and I cradled her in my arms and crooned grief and sympathy for her. After a long, long day, she opened her eyes again.

"I hurt," she said.

"You will be all right."

"My head." She put her hand up and winced.

"It is not broken."

"I feel . . ." And she slept.

She was dizzy for a few days, during which we made camp by the stream and she constantly wanted me to hold her, which, as she felt better, led to other things, and, finally, laughing, I accused her of pretending to be dizzy so that we would not walk but stay in camp to do the together closeness.

She smiled, but then she shuddered. "When I saw the dragon . . ."

"You saw it?"

"Then I felt the pain and there was a moment when I was alive before I died and in that moment I knew regret."

"I know," I said. "I would have felt it, too, for I would have died, my Mar, without telling you that you are my true pairmate."

"Truly?" I had explained to her the ways of our people, that pairs mate for life and two lives are as one.

"Truly."

"My regret, too, was that I had not spoken," she said.

"Speak now, then," I said.

"I hesitate."

"We are pairmates. You may speak anything."

"But I may be wrong." She clung to me. "Oh, I do not want to be wrong."

"Between pairmates, nothing is wrong except the giving of pain," I said.

"It is that I have not blooded for three moons," she said.

I digested this information, nodding. Thinking of all the implications, remembering the deformed baby which an inbreeder had killed by smashing its head against a tree.

"Perhaps I am merely old, for in old women the blooding stops," she said.

"At fifteen, no, sixteen summers?" I asked.

"I will be happy if I am right," she said. "Will you, Eban?" She gazed at me from behind long lashes, her face fearful.

"It will be a son," I said. "We will call it after my father."

"And you are happy?"

"Yes," I said. But I could think of nothing except that deformed thing which died even before it lived, of the sickness in Mar's people, of the warning tingle which came, ever so faintly, from her very bones. It is forbidden to mate with the inbreeders of the lower slopes. Another sin for the head of Eban, Killer of His People. Now I was taking the taint, the sickness, into the very home of my kind.

We circled the field of the dragon. His path lay through a valley, and he was in the center, commanding a view of the entire valley and the ridges surrounding it, and had I been inclined to kill, I would have been sore tested to approach that one, for he was well placed.

Within a moon Mar's belly was swollen, and she was happy. We saw signs of people, but I skirted them. I did not want to be seen by the true men of the hills, without hair, in my present condition, with a hairy inbreeder woman as my companion. But I had forgotten the skills of my people. As we made our way up a valley, leading into the hills, making camps beside a clear and cold stream, living on the plenty of the hills, I walked into an ambush without realizing it. I had become spoiled by the easy life among the lesser men. I saw, suddenly, two men leap into the clearing in front of me.

"Ho, hairy one," one of them said.

"I am Eban the Hunter, son of Egan, of the family of Strabo the Strongarm of the northern hills," I said, bowing in politeness, my hardax dangling in front of me.

"He knows the form," one man said.

"Haired," the other said. "He lies."

"I have hair, but I am a man," I said. "I have killed dragons, for which I have proof, with your permission."

"Ha," said a mountain man.

I took that for permission. I took the necklace of dragon's guts from my pack. Mar refused to wear it. I tossed it onto the ground at the feet of the mountain men.

"Ha," they said, together. "How can it be true, from a hairy one?"

"It is a curse," I said. "And I have suffered for it. But I have flown, and I have seen the killbird."

"No inbreeder talks so," said one of them.

"I beg only that we be allowed to cross your land," I said. "We seek nothing, save living room, and we hope to find it in the western hills, where our hair will give no offense."

"That is for the family head to decide," said one.

"Understood. May I beg to speak with him?"

"Follow."

"Ho," said the other. "First I test. Lay down your bow and hardax, hairy one."

I obeyed his orders. He came close, so close that he could have felt the warning had he been so close to Mar, but he did not test Mar, only me. And he said, "It is true. He is not of the inbreeders."

We followed the two mountain men into a clean and tidy village of hidehouses. It was the family of Stoneskull the Leftarm. He reminded me so much of Strabo that I was saddened. We were surrounded by the people, in front of Stoneskull's hidehouse, and given leave to speak. I repeated my desire for safe passage to the west.

"There be dragons," Stoneskull said.

"I am Eban, slayer of dragons," I said, presenting him with one strand of my dragon's-gut necklace. There was an oohing and a moan of approval.

"We will hear your story," Stoneskull said, and with feasting and rhythm from the drum, I told of my slaying of both the lion and the dragon and, for the first time, never even having told it to Mar, the tale of my leading the killbird to slay my family. There was a moan of sympathy.

"It is true, God has seen fit to try you," Stoneskull said. "I think you have suffered enough, and, although you are haired, you may, should you choose, live in our lands."

But not, I noted in their village. "You are generous, honorable father," I said. "But we seek solitude to live with our curse in peace."

"I grant you permission to traverse our lands, but I warn you that beyond the rocky dome there be dragons so deadly that no man returns."

We spent the night in the village, sleeping in the open, for no one was willing to give hospitality to haired ones, and then set out. The hills seemed to be thickly populated with families. But they were all offshoots of the Stoneskull family, so that word went ahead of us and we were welcomed with food and fireside in camps between a series of ridges which led ever deeper into the mountains. I became Eban the Storyteller, and there were times when I could hear Mar giggle as, to add entertainment value, I embellished our adventures.

But at last we were below the rocky dome, and beyond it, as we were constantly warned, were dragons of the fiercest disposition.

Mar was big in the belly when we made the last climb. To her everlasting credit, she did not complain, nor did she question my decisions. She, too, felt the shame of being considered a freak and wanted to find a valley of our own, a place where we could have our child and, dream though it was, start our own family, a family of hairy ones in the midst of the people.

A mist crept over us as we climbed. The going was easy, for although the dome was the highest in that part of the mountains, the dome from which I flew, that last time, reached to the clouds. The summit was barren, rocky. Huge boulders joined each other in a line along the crest. I approached them cautiously and peered over into the valley beyond, a narrow cleft between two ridged backs. I saw neither dragon nor the white bones of the dead. Nor did I see sign as we went down into the cleft, started the climb of the opposite side, gained the top of the ridge and looked out over ridges descending toward the west.

"The dragons of these hills," I told Mar, "are like the dragons of the east, often told but seldom seen."

"I pray so," she said.

The days were shortening. Soon it would be time to build a hidehouse, to make a clearing, to store provisions for the winter. I felt like a new man, home in my mountains, the air clean, the temperatures cool. I studied the ridges ahead of me and saw, the second ridge over, that there was space for what should be a nice valley. "There," I said, pointing. We took a leisurely two days to make the journey, I taking note of a dam of the swimmers and promising Mar a winter garment of their warm hides. I saw bear sign. I began to look upon that valley, which now lay just over the next ridge, as my home, and I prayed that the tales of the dragons had kept it free of men.

I was to find one obstacle. As we climbed, I came upon a dragon's path of a type not known to me. The dragon had lain down two lines of dragon stuff which lay, bleeding and twisted, atop a little mound which extended alongside the ridge. It was evident that the path was long unused. In places there were slides and the lines of dragon stuff were buried. It made for easy walking, and it seemed to point toward the top of the ridge, so we followed—to see, as we rounded an outcrop of rock with a drop of two arrow flights to the bed of a rocky stream below, the strangest dragon of my experience. I leaped back. Mar was behind me, and dragon's teeth shattered the rock outcrop and hummed off into the air over the long drop.

"We must go back," she said.

"We shall see."

I crawled and peered around the outcrop. The dragon lay, half curled, in the curve of ridge, long, bleeding with ancient blood, one large eye on its head looking directly down the path toward me. The dragon was segmented, and I could see that his body was connected by a backbone, low, and at the end of the segments I could see space between them, except where the backbone connected, down low, I considered. The dragon was blocking the way to my unseen valley, but he was stupid, like my first dragon, for he had chosen his lair below a cliff which rose above him. I determined to test him, to find his capabilities. The path in front of us was littered with rock fall and obviously unused. Indeed, the path to his very head was the same, and, as I examined him, I suspected that he was unable, for some reason, to move, for there were no fresh tracks and things grew in the pathway. Was he mortally wounded and lying there to die, taking eternity to do it?

I took off my pack, took out my sleepskin, held it on my longbow and suspended it beyond the outcrop and did not manage to jerk it back until, with a blast of

Why not? Take 4 for 10¢ now
WITH MEMBERSHIP IN THE SCIENCE FICTION BOOK CLUB

An Extraordinary Offer

What a way to get acquainted with these science fiction greats. Browse through the list of books on this page and choose any 4 for just 10¢. An extraordinary sample of science fiction all in one package.

How The
Science Fiction Book Club Works:

When your application for membership is accepted, you'll receive your introductory package of four books for just 10¢, plus shipping and handling. You may examine them in your home, and if not completely satisfied, return them within ten days—membership will be cancelled and you'll owe nothing.

About every 4 weeks (14 times a year), we'll send you the Club's bulletin, *Things to Come*, describing the 2 coming Selections and a variety of Alternate choices. If you want both Selections, you need do nothing; they'll be shipped automatically.

If you don't want a Selection, or prefer an Alternate, or no book at all, just fill out the convenient form always provided, and return it to us by the date specified.

We allow you at least ten days for making your decision. If you do not receive the form in time to respond within 10 days, and receive an unwanted Selection, you may return it at our expense.

As a member you need take only 4 Selections or Alternates during the coming year. You may resign any time thereafter, or remain a member as long as you wish. One of the two Selections each month is only $2.49. Other Selections are slightly higher, but always much less than Publishers Editions. A shipping and handling charge is added to each shipment. Send no money. Mail postage-paid card today!

Science Fiction Book Club
Dept. UR869, Garden City, N.Y. 11530

Yes, I want to join
The Science Fiction Book Club

Please accept me as a member. I agree to the membership plan as described above. Send me the 4 books whose numbers I have indicated below, and bill me just 10¢ plus shipping and handling. I agree to take 4 additional books at low club prices in the coming year and may resign any time thereafter. SFBC books are selections for mature readers.

Mr. _____
Ms.
                    (Please print)

Address _____ Apt. # ____

City_____ State____ Zip _____
Order not valid without signature. If under 18, parent must sign.

_____

The Science Fiction Book Club offers its own complete hardbound editions sometimes altered in size to fit special presses and save members even more. Members accepted in U.S.A. and Canada only. Canadian members will be serviced from Toronto. Offer slightly different in Canada.

51-S141

sound and buzzing, teeth shredded it. The dragon had no shortage of teeth, despite his obvious age.

"Please, let's go back," Mar begged.

"It is only one dragon," I said, "and it spits teeth only from its middle." Indeed, I had observed that as the dragon ruined my sleepskin. Three heads on its middle, on one of the separate segments of his body, turned and spat as I tested him once again, watching closely. The other segments had eyes, but they seemed to be of the sort which were on the cave of the giants, eyes without the deadly burning fires. I made a few more tests, just to be sure, and there was no burst of fire, only the teeth which made little popping sounds as they passed close by, outside the protecting outcrop.

"We will kill him and rid the mountains of him," I said.

"He will kill us," Mar said.

"No. Now, here is what you must do." I told her, and I left her there. The year with me had given her courage. I climbed to the top of the ridge and made my way carefully to a point overlooking the dragon's middle. There I positioned myself. Then, for I wanted more information, I shrilled out a signal to Mar. She heard and extended the tattered sleepskin on a stick. I watched. The three heads jerked and spat, and as they spat I stood in the open and yelled at the dragon. Immediately one head started turning, and I dived for cover. Yes, I knew then that the heads could turn individually and that I would have to work carefully.

I went for Mar, took her to a safe distance, made our camp. At the sun, she insisting upon going with me, I went to the top of the ridge and studied the situation. This one was an alert dragon, sending his heads searching at the sound of my movements, hailing his spat teeth into the thick trees around us.

In any forest there is an ample supply of deadwood, unless fire has passed recently, and this forest, although not overly thick, was littered with deadwood. First I cut green saplings, and, crawling on my belly and using rocks for cover, hearing the song of the spat teeth around and over me, but staying behind the protecting stones, I built a sort of hold, a bed of green saplings braced against rocks and half suspended over the cliff. Then, that part of it finished, the rest was easier. I was able to toss deadwood and debris onto my platform from the safety of the cover of the trees until, by nightfall, I had a huge pile. The weight of it sagged the saplings which held it. Since I wanted to be sure of seeing all of the action, I waited for morning, and then, with the sun, I tossed a burning brand into the huge pile of deadwood. The resulting fire spread quickly until, smoke reaching for the skies, there was a huge blaze which ate through the supporting saplings and sent the entire blazing mass down the cliff. It lodged exactly where I'd planned, against the living portion of the dragon. Now I followed through, sending the largest dead logs I could roll tumbling down the cliff into the blazing fire, until, after a morning's sweaty work, there was a heap of burning logs beside the dragon, which, as I'd suspected, could not move. From a place of safety we watched as the fire burned hotter and hotter, the thick logs blazing, the flames licking high on the dragon's sides. We waited. Once a head turned and sent an aimless spit of teeth into the air, and then all three heads went into motion. As we watched the dragon, which was obviously in pain, there was a flash of light followed by a boom of thunder louder than the summer storms, and the dragon burst as a green nut bursts when thrown into a bed of glowing embers. One by one his segments, the chaos of God following his body in two directions, from middle to front, from middle to back, burst with the thunder, and I knew great fear for both myself and Mar, for dragon flesh began to rain down everywhere. Only the fact that we were in dense tree cover saved us from injury or death as dragonskin fell, some of it sizzling hot, all around us, bouncing down through the branches, knocking away branches and leaves and needles.

When all was quiet I ventured a look over the cliff. Only the dragon's head survived, and a segment of his tail. I led Mar down to the scene of his death, and there were bits of skin for the picking, some jagged and excellent for hardaxes. A fire was burning in the dragon's dead head, and as we watched it spread, apparently feeding on stored blood, which leaked and burned and engulfed the head and left, after a day of burning, only blackened shells of the dragon's head. In the shattered tail we found sharp pieces of eye, good for scraping and for decoration, and, most valuable, chair things covered with a sort of hide which was soft and warm. I told Mar we would come back for it to make her pretty skirts. And there was a treasure house of dragonskin all around me. Our new life would be started in ease and richness, and should I desire, I could march back to the people of the Stoneskull families and trade for many buythings with the skin pieces.

Now, however, I wanted to see my valley.

We walked down the rotted and broken dragon's path and came to a curious place where the path went into the mountain, into a blackness lined with a sort of white stone or bone. Eban the curious looked in and saw light at the far end. It seemed to extend under the ridge and come out the other side.

"I will not," Mar said.

"The dragon is dead."

"You go if you must, and leave your child fatherless and your pairmate lonely."

"That would be a sadness," I said, grinning. "So we go together."

So, unwillingly, she came, clutching my hand tightly. There was nothing. The dragon's hole simply went under the mountain and came out the other side, and we looked down upon the sweetest valley I'd seen since leaving the Valley of Clean Water. Gods of man, it was beautiful. It was a perfect bowl, and all around the hill rose to almost uniform height, with no gap that I could see. The dragon's path went around the inside of the ridge and spiraled downward toward the valley floor, I was too eager to take the long way. I led Mar down the slope.

I noted a stream cascading down the side of the slope and knew that somewhere there had to be a way out of the valley, otherwise the entire bowl would be a lake. I would find the outlet for the stream later. I would explore every stone, every tree, for the valley was mine, mine and my pairmate's and our unborn son's.

With an eye toward permanence, I found a pleasant knoll near the stream and selected a site high enough to prevent flooding when the snows melted.

"Here we will build our house," I told Mar. I had one fresh deerhide, and there were signs of plenty of game. I left Mar beside a fire at the new homesite and went walking, took a huge stag near the camp, skinned him, and put Mar to work preparing the skin. We had fresh meat roasted over the fire and slept entwined to wake with a feeling of joy and anticipation.

My valley was not as small as it first appeared. It took us several days to familiarize ourselves with it. There were wild fruit trees on the southern edge which offered a bounty, since the fruit was at its ripest; and there was an abundance of small game. I had, I discovered, my own farm of swimmers to be harvested as needed for clothing. Now, however, the main object was to finish the hidehouse. To gather the material I hunted alone and found, at the western end of the valley, the outlet of our stream. A natural cleft in the rock wall had been breached, and the stream tumbled through a narrow ravine with towering hills on either side, the depths of the gorge seldom seeing the sun, so narrow was it. I made a tentative probe into the ravine, wading and noting that fat fish lay in shallow pools. I was no more than an arrow's flight into the ravine when I saw the warning gleam of whiteness. From long habit I froze and then sought cover. Dragons in that deep and narrow ravine? Not likely. And yet, as I looked carefully, I saw another and another pile of weathered white bones of death, and I set out to study the situation. I saw nothing. There was no space for a dragon's path, and I began to think that the animal had been a victim of a lion or a bear. However, I knew that rashness is danger, so I did not plunge into the ravine, but, rather, retreated and sought to climb the hill to the north to get an overall view of the ravine. I startled a deer, and, since deerhide was my objective, I loosed an arrow which took the beast in the shoulder in a nonfatal spot. Panicked, in dire pain, no doubt, the poor animal bolted, saw me, and turned to run into the ravine, splashing along the bed of the stream. He had gone only a short distance when, with a chatter of horrible proportions, at least two dragons, one on either side of the ravine and high up on the hills, began to spit teeth in such a hail that the deer was slain in midleap.

I saw the flash of an eye, high near the top. I did not like that development. Dragons on the hills. They could, it seemed, have a view of the entire valley. However, both Mar and I had walked near, within range of a dragon's teeth, and had lived. It was a puzzle. I began to climb the slope, finding the going tough as the side of the hill steepened, and kept an eye out for the telltale signs of the bones of death. There were none. I made a slow approach to the spot from which I had seen the gleam of an eye, and, in the dense growth, was closer than I wanted to be when I saw the bloodstained hide of a dragon showing through the trees. I crept close. This was a peculiar dragon, I found, with no feet. His body was half a globe, sitting on the ground, and his head was not eyed all around.

There were eyes on the front side, facing the ravine, and holes from which the dragon had spat teeth. I studied how to kill the beast, to rid my valley of him. Since he was on top of the hill, I could not roll rocks down on him, and that left only fire. However, to burn him meant exposing myself, and I had little inclination to do that.

But behind the dragon were no bones of death. Looking past him into the ravine I could see several white spots. Could he not, then, turn his head? To test him I exposed myself, ready to leap for cover. There was no action from the dragon. I taunted and jeered and crept ever closer until I was close enough to cast stones which rang off his tough hide. He seemed not to notice. However, when I threw large stones past him his head jerked and followed their roll down the steep side of the ravine. A peculiar dragon, indeed. I crept to his side and put my hand on his cold and bloodstained hide. He did not seem to know I was there. I began to gather dry wood and built a fire at his back, stacked it with logs and went back into the trees to watch. The fire burned for a long time and I kept awaiting the blast of his bursting, but when there were only embers his hide was blackened by smoke but intact. He was a tough one. I knew that he had a mate on the opposite side of the ravine, and keeping behind him, I began to search out the other dragon. At last, hidden in underbrush, I saw the sun reflect off an eye, and then, to my concern, I saw another reflection a bit farther down the ravine, still at the top of the hills, however. I scouted on my side and came upon a second dragon like the first, unable to turn his head to the rear. I didn't like it at all. I continued to the top of the hill on the south side of the ravine and saw, ahead, the white bones of death. A bit of careful scouting found a line of dragons extending along the top of the ridge, and, before night fell and forced me to return to a worried Mar, I had determined that on all the hills surrounding my valley there was a line of the footless dragons, all facing outward, as if to protect the valley. Another day's scouting made me realize how lucky we were to have approached the valley through the dragon's hole in the mountain, for everywhere else the approaches were guarded by dragons which had, this proved by testing, an ample store of teeth to spit.

It was a puzzle, but the abundance of game proved to me that the dragons did not spit teeth into the valley.

"It is not all for the bad," I told Mar. "We will be assured of our privacy. It is unlikely that anyone will be dropping in unexpectedly over the hills."

"But why are there so many?" she asked.

"Who knows, with dragons?" I asked.

"What do they eat?"

"Dragons slay for malice or sport or for some dragon reason unknown to man," I said, "not for food, for when they kill, the food is wasted."

"We must go and find a place without dragons," she said.

"Soon it will be winter and soon you will be very large. I like this valley and it is safe."

"Perhaps they are only toying with us," she said, "and will turn their deadly mouths on us without warning."

"I have examined them closely. They seem to be rooted to the ground like large trees. I dug half my body length beside one and found only more hide hidden below the ground. No, they cannot turn."

So the hidehouse took shape. And soon the cold came with the nights, and Mar was growing larger. We ate of the plenty of the hunt and of the dried meats and nuts and spent the last summer nights with our fire vented through the roof of our hidehouse talking of what we would teach our son.

Mar was restless and liked to walk about. She liked the stream, and we spent lovely days exploring it, wading in the rapidly cooling water, lying in hiding to ob-

serve the swimmers at their task of storing branches for
their winter food. Their dam had created a sizable but
shallow lake near the valley's center, and there was
thick growth along the margins of the lake. We pene-
trated the bogs looking for frogs one day and made another discovery. There, hidden from view by the dense
growth encouraged by the shallow water, was an island. We gained the dry ground and walked through a
lovely glade shaded by tall trees, and suddenly there
was something ahead. I pushed Mar into cover behind
a tree and waited for movement. Then I went forward,
crawling from tree to tree, and saw a low mound of
strange material, with no eyes and no mouths on the
side from which I approached. Now if there was so
huge a dragon in the center of my valley that was
something entirely different.

I crawled closer and saw that creepers and underbrush concealed a thing much like the shape of the
dragons on the hills around the valley, but as I circled
it I still saw no eyes or mouths. Not until I was all the
way to the other side did anything come into view, and
then it was a plate much like the plates on dragons or
on the dragon's cave far to the east where the small
dragons ate grass, mended broken eyes and put out
fires.

I had often thought of that wondrous cave and the
treasures therein and my greed sent me forward to examine the plate close up. It was sunken into the skin of
the thing. I threw stones at it and nothing happened. I
went back for Mar.

Mar did not feel adventurous and wanted to leave. I
reminded her of the treasures—I still used the dragonskin knives—we'd left in the dragon's cave to the east.
I stood before the plate and nothing happened. I felt it
with my hands. It was cold and bloodstained. When I
touched a place, a sort of pimple at the height of my
head, there was a hum and I leaped away. The plate
swung inward slowly, making a creaking noise like a

moving dragon, letting dirt and roots tumble inward as it opened. We watched for a long time, and the plate began to close, but was prevented from closing entirely by the dirt and roots which blocked it at the bottom. I ventured forward and peered within. It was black inside. I touched the pimple again and the plate swung open and the sun came out inside. I was startled, but remembered the same magic in the dragon's cave to the east. I peered in. Inside was a cave, round, clean, the air smelling fresh, well lighted. I stuck my head in farther, looking for treasures, and saw disappointingly little. The floor was smooth and warm to my feet, but the room was without treasures, barren. The walls were of the same material as the floor and felt warm to the touch. In fact, the entire cave was pleasantly warm with the temperature of a fine day at the start of the growing season.

I tried to get Mar to join me, but she refused. I stepped inside. The plate closed behind me, but I was not concerned, for the dirt and roots blocking it left enough space for me to escape. The sun stayed out, lighting the cave. I put my hands on a pimple on the inside of the plate and it swung open.

Since there were no treasures, we left the place, but it remained in my thoughts as the days grew chill and Mar's belly swelled. We awoke one morning to find a covering of snow.

"I will see the warm cave again," I told Mar. She went with me. The place was the same, the plate still blocked by dirt and debris. A breath of pleasantly warm air came from the opening. Inside it was the same, and the temperature was delightful, a pleasant warmth after the cold of the outdoors.

I cleared away the dirt and roots from the plate and experimented with it repeatedly. It always opened to the pressure of my hand from within or without.

"I will sleep here," I said.

"No," she said.

"Just me, at first, to be sure that it is safe in the night."

"If you will be so foolish I will come with you," she said, and I could not convince her to spend the night in our hidehouse.

We slept. An amazing thing happened. The sun shown brightly until we were cuddled in our sleepskins and our eyes closed, and then it dimmed until there was only a glow, as on a night of the full moon, but if we arose the sun came out again. After a while we tired of testing the magic and slept, warm and comfortable.

Not even Mar, after that night, protested when we moved into the cave on the island in the middle of the swimmer's lake. I left the hidehouse, flap closed, in case of future need, but moved our food supplies and possessions into the cave. The first big snow of the winter came, and we had no need for fire, except in the outdoors, where I built a lean-to against the side of our cave for cooking. We did not make the mistake of building a fire in the cave, remembering the white rain which fell and clung to us in the other cave far to the east. Soon Mar was coming and going with confidence, the plate always opening when a hand was placed on the pimple inside or out. With no need to gather firewood for warmth, only for cooking. I had little to do except hunt in the snow for fresh meat, which remained plentiful. Inside it was cozy and we were never wet and we played the game of feeling baby kick. I would place my ear on Mar's belly and my son would oblige by punching a knee or an elbow against the skin, and I'd find myself laughing in delight.

I had only one concern, and that was the lack of a woman to aid when the time came. Mar said not to worry. She had aided in the delivery of many babies and would tell me what to do, doing most of it herself. I wanted to journey out the dragon's hole and find a family and borrow a midwife for the necessary length of time, and she protested.

"It is our valley," she said. "Ours and ours alone. I don't want others here."

To while away the long winter days I started the construction of wings. In that remote place, flying from the top of one of the hills into the center of the valley, I estimated, could be done without attracting a killbird. Mar had never seen wings and was fascinated but fearful when I told her my plans to celebrate the birth of our son with a praise, a flight dedicated to God and the gods of man.

It was a long project. The hollowed wood had to be properly dried. The hides had to be scraped and scraped to a thinness. But there was plenty of room inside our house. (We had come to think of it as ours and were quite at home there.)

Snow lay deep in the valley, and I had to chop holes in the ice to get water. I carried it in a pouch made of leather. Mar's time was near. I began to spend more and more time with her inside the house, and thus quite often I became bored as she napped to prepare herself for her trial. One day, out of sheer idleness, I began to measure the distance around the house, using my hands, counting as I palmed my way along the wall, my hands at the height of my face. It was then that I noticed, for the first time, little protrusions on the wall at a height just above my eyes. They were spaced here and there and were, I decided, much like those which caused our plate to open and close.

Of course, Eban the curious had to investigate. I put my palm on a protrusion and pushed, leaping back with a cry of alarm when a plate opened in the seamless hide and left me expecting to see the eyes of a dragon or worse inside. Mar was still sleeping. I lived. I crept back and looked into the hole and saw a curious bowllike thing of some hard material. I felt it and as I extended my hand over it a stream of water

gushed and gurgled into the bowl. After I recovered
from my shock I tried it again. It was wondrous. The
water was warmer than the waters of summer, as warm
as the water of the hot spring of the mountains from
which the family of Strabo had moved into the Valley
of Clean Waters. I tasted the water and it was good,
but warm. Not really pleasant for drinking. It was,
however, lovely for washing. I dawdled my hands into
an accumulation of it in the bowl and when I took my
hands out the water drained away with a gurgle and a
rush of warm air came, startling me, but drying my
hands when I had courage to go back and try again.

So. Our house had hidden treasures after all. I
moved to the next protrusion, pushed it, watched a
plate slide back into the skin, and there was a fountain
of clear water jetting into the air and falling back into
a bowl. I tested this water and it was icy, like the
waters of a mountain stream, and quite delicious. Unable to contain myself any longer, I woke Mar and
showed her the wonders, coaxing her into washing and
drying her hands at the bowl and tasting the cool water
of the fountain. The next plate was much larger, almost as large as the plate which gave access to our
house. It opened into a small cave which contained
things we did not understand. There was a strangely
shaped chair which had a hole in it and contained
water, and there was a little cave closed off by
eyes which moved as I touched them to reveal a place
of hard material. I stepped in and was immediately wet
thoroughly by a rain of water which came from above,
and before I could leap out there was a rain of some
sweet-smelling slick stuff which I could not get off my
face, clothing, hands. Since I was wet and since the
water still rained in the small cave, I stepped back inside. The water was warm as summer, and after another spraying of the slick, sweet-smelling stuff the
water cleansed me and my clothing. The warm air
which blew from all around after the water stopped

dried me, but not my clothing, so I left off my exploration to put on another skin and then went on to the next protrusion. This was the most wonderful of all.

As I pushed the pimple I heard a hum and a section of the wall slid away to reveal a small and lighted cave. Chair things were placed around a flat surface which stood on legs, and when I climbed onto one of the chair things to better see the surface of the flat thing, which was shiny and rather pretty, a delightful aroma filled the cave, a plate opened and out came a thing with steaming bowls atop. The aroma was both meaty and something else. I put my finger into one bowl and licked it. The taste was strange, but when I used one of the eating things, made of dragonskin and shaped much like the spoons which the old men carve for family use out of wood, it was edible and interesting.

We went no further that day. After the bowl with the hot and delicious liquid there came from the plate a dish of meat which was so well cooked, so delicious, that I ate much, and Mar overcame her nervousness to join me. The good things which issued from that plate kept us there until my belly protruded almost as much as Mar's and she could eat not another bite, not even the delicious things which were white and light and tasted as sweet as the stickiness of the stinging bees. As long as we sat and waited the magic continued, and when I could eat no more I went outside into the snow, put my finger down my throat, voided my stomach, and went back to begin again. Not since I was a child and ate myself to sickness on finding a bee tree did I do such sinful gluttony, but the supply seemed to be never-ending and the variety was amazing, although some things I could not stomach, mainly the soft and strange-tasting things which I suspected—and checked carefully for the warning tingles—were products of vegetation.

Glutted, sated, we slept. We ate the next morning and all that day, and only then did I move to the next and, I found, the last visible protrusion on the wall of our house. I pushed it, not knowing what wonders to expect, and the plate opened, as had all the others, to reveal only a white eye on the wall of the small cave, a hard chair thing, and, in front of the chair thing and below the eye, a flat but solid thing which was rooted on the floor.

I was disappointed. I explored the remainder of the walls and found nothing of interest. Only then did I come back to the last little cave and push and probe. I could, I thought, break the eye. I tapped it with my hardax, and it was strong. There seemed to be something over the eye, unlike the eyes of, for example, dragons or the cave of the giants to the east. I tried harder, and no matter how hard I hit the eye I could not dent or break the strong, clear material which protected it. To think about it, I climbed up into the chair thing, and immediately there was a hum and the eye came to life and I scrambled for my own life. The eye glowed and there appeared in it a series of little lines, running from one side to the other. When I determined that there was no danger, I went back and sat in the chair, and the lines appeared and faded. On close examination the lines were made up of individual little things, looking somewhat like strange bugs. But they did not move. Only the lines changed from time to time. Then, after a while, the lines went away and a star appeared. The star was in the middle of the eye, and then the flat thing in front of the chair came to life, showing in a glow of color a bunch of things, stars, dots, circles, squares. The star on the eye glowed and faded, as did the star which was one of the things on the flat surface. I reached out and touched the glowing star on the flat surface, and the star on the eye faded to be replaced by a circle, and a circle glowed on the flat surface. I touched the circle there, and the circle went away to be replaced.

Mar wanted to try. It was a fun game. A thing

would appear in the eye and on the flat surface, and when you touched the thing on the flat surface the thing in the eye would go away and be replaced with another image. We played for a long time, and then the pictures went away. A single line appeared on the eye. I pushed my finger at the single line which matched it on the flat surface, and two lines appeared. I pushed my finger at the two lines, and three, and so on until we'd counted to twenty in this manner.

Now one line appeared on the eye again. I pushed one line. But the next thing was not two lines but a thing with a curve at the top and a flat line at the bottom. There was nothing like it on the flat surface. However, the two-line picture was glowing, and I pushed it and the curved thing went away to be replaced with a thing with two curves and the three lines glowed on the flat surface. I didn't like that game as well, but played it, finding that it passed the cold winter day, but when the pictures on the eye started switching into random appearances of the things with curves and different shapes I found that I could not remember how many lines to push to cause them to go away until, after a while, the flat surface would glow.

Mar, who counted only on her fingers and toes, found the game boring, but as the days passed I found myself returning to it. I came to the realization, at last, that the eye was trying to tell me something. For example, the thing with double curves was a sign for three, only instead of having to make three slash marks you only had to make the one double-curved mark. It was interesting and opened up an entirely new line of thinking to me.

As the winter deepened around us and game became scarce and the creek was frozen down to within a couple of hands of the bottom, we played our games with the eye and ate at the magic cave and drank our cool water from the magic fountain and Mar's belly told her it was time. She instructed me and prepared herself, and all through one long night she groaned with the pains, and then it was indeed time, for she was heaving and moaning and telling me how to help, and I saw the bulge of something between her legs, and she cried out, strained. I held the outcoming thing, wet and sticky, gingerly, and then with one great heave it was over and I held a squirming bundle of muck and wetness in my hands, frightened, not knowing what to do in spite of all Mar's careful teachings. She took it from me, cleaned away the muck, hung the little thing by its heels and patted it, and there was a sound which caused me to laugh for joy, the protesting, feeble cry of the newborn. Then I was examining it with a beating heart, looking for the terror, finding only perfect little tiny feet and hands and the shriveled little sign that it was, indeed, a son.

Then, suddenly, Mar tensed and moaned and I knew more fear, for I remembered the time she'd helped a woman deliver and one of the babies had been a monster. But the second came quickly, and I cleaned it myself, Mar resting from her labors. I bit the cord which held it to its mother and spanked the little rump, and the little girl baby bawled louder than her brother had.

Two perfect and lovely little babies with skulls of a thickness which pleased me and perfectly shaped heads.

Gods of man, the joy of it.

6

There was no joy in me, however, when I aborted my flight of praise to God. I had carried my wings to the top of a hill behind the guarding line of dragons. I positioned Mar and the babies near the swimmers' lake, where I would conclude my brief flight, having been in air only a short time, not nearly so long as even a ceremonial flight back in my own country with my own people and nothing like as long as Logan and I soared before the killbird came to kill my family. I had too much to live for, you see. I wanted no risk.

I had cleared a runway. All was in readiness. Snow lay soft and deep in my valley, but the sun was warm and the day splendid. I waved to Mar, off in the distance, made my run, leaped, my heart soaring as I felt the wings bite air and lift. And I had not been in the air for nine wing lengths—I could see the symbol for nine, a round head on a little curve—before I looked up and saw, coming out of the sky directly above me, the white streak. Never had a killbird been so vigilant.

"Oh, God," I cried, and looked down for a landing spot. I was over the steep side of the hill with nothing below me but trees, and the killbird was streaking, and already, as I dipped my wings and started to circle, I could hear his bellowing roar, and I knew that I was a dead man unless I reached ground quickly. Better to risk a broken head or a twisted limb, which could be healed, than to vanish forever in a roar as had Strabo and my family. I could see the gleam of the killbird's hide as I lowered a wing further and slipped down faster and faster, looking for a minute hole in the solid greenery of the treetops, praying, thinking of Mar alone and my two children, boy and girl. Roar and flash as I glanced up, the nose of the killbird pointed at me and the trees coming up, and then I went down between two tops, the wings caught and ripped, the braces breaking with little snaps and the whole world a roar as the killbird flashed by overhead, arcing, making me think for one horrible moment that he was following me into the trees. Then I had time to think only of myself as I fell away from the broken and crumpled wings.

I went down, down, rolled into a knot. I hoped the snow was deep and there were no rocks and then I hit and was still conscious, but rolling down the steep slope with the harness tangled around me until I fetched up against a tree with a bang which made me see white spots in front of my eyes, and I could hear the roar of the killbird diminishing as he climbed, and then I saw his streak, climbing high, back into the sun from where he had come. I was alive.

I was bruised and my right leg was sore, but I was alive. I walked through the snow to find Mar coming, carrying little Egan and Margan on her back in their carry pouches. She threw herself on me and we fell into the snow, and Egan started crying.

"You must never fly again," she wailed.

"I think not," I said. "Not with alert killbirds like that one."

I grew lazy. With food there for the asking, all we had to do was sit at the flat surface in the eating cave. What need to hunt? We had food for dozens. We could have fed an entire family, and I found myself thinking wistfully of my old family, wondering about Yuree and Yorerie the Butcher and all the rest. It is funny how, when you've been away for a long time, you find yourself wondering about people whom you didn't even particularly like. Logan, for example. Was he a good hunter? Had he become pairmate to Yuree?

One day I used one of the dragonskin knives, honed to sharpness, to scrape away my hair on face and skull, and Mar laughed at me. I did not dare tell her that I was thinking of paying a visit to the people, perhaps not my own, but one of the families allied with Stoneskull. There was a problem, but it was not an immediate one. I would have two young ones for pairmating in the future. That, I told myself, was my reason for thinking of people.

The life of ease and plenty was making me soft, and I grew irritable and restless. After the nights started getting shorter, but winter still held the mountains under a fine snow accumulation, I told Mar that I would hunt. She, too, was spoiled, by having me with her at all times. I told her that it was the duty of a man to hunt and that the hunt, especially in the winter, meant that I would be gone for more than one day. She wailed, but I was firm.

I have to admit that I was ready, after spending one night in the open, in the cold, shivering in my sleepskin with a fire to cheer me, to go back to the comfort of the always-warm cave. I did not yield to the temptation, however. I made one trip around my valley and saw that all was well. The deer were wintering as well as could be expected. There were no large predators in my valley, so the only enemy the deer had to survive was winter itself.

I determined to make a scout outside the valley and spent several days making a wide circle around, up hill and down valley, always on the alert, once or twice coming up on my valley's protective hills merely to test the alertness of the guardian dragons. They never failed to show me that they were eternally watchful. I found a bear's den on a mountainside, smelling it out by the escape of air from a vent, and toyed with the idea of making Mar a gift of a bearskin. However, I knew from folklore that sometimes bears sleep two in a cave, and I didn't feel it wise to try to take on two angry bears. Bears are very ill-natured, when they're awakened in the midst of their winter's sleep.

I was pleased by the beauty and the plenty of our mountains. The dragons of my hills had kept man far away, so that for at least two or three days' march on any side of my valley there was nothing but the wild and unpeopled forest, streams frozen under their winter blankets, swimmer dams, the signs of many deer, the winter nests of climbers and the tracks of more than one lion. There were no dragons save those which guarded my valley, and they were no danger as long as one did not try to enter the valley over the hills but came in and out through the dragon's hole.

My loneliness was emphasized by the quiet of winter, the vastness of the mountains, and the total absence of my fellow man. And I thought ahead to the time when Egan and Margan would come of age. I dreamed of having four, even five fine premen asking for my daughter. From where would they come? Here around my valley was an ideal range for an entire family, several families, and there were no men and would be none when my children came of age. As I lay in my sleepskins with a cheery fire going I saw an ugly vision, my two children inbreeding to produce the footless horror I had seen, so long ago, on the plains of the inbreeders.

With new determination, I marched quickly back to the valley, where I was greeted with joy by Mar. I told her my decision. I would venture forth into the lands of man and tell of the wonders of our mountains. I would sing the praises of that unspoiled and unhunted country. When man came, with me as guide, we would be friends, but not a part of the family, and then when the children were of age there would be pairmates for them.

I would set out immediately and return with the spring thaws.

"You will not leave me alone," she said. "I will go with you."

"And carry two infants through the winter snows?"

"Then we will wait for the thaw and go together," she said.

At first I thought to strike her for defying me, but we had a special relationship, Mar and I, engendered by our having none other save ourselves. We were alone in a vast and deserted range by ourselves, and I concluded that it was not female arrogance for her to dispute my plans, merely a dependence upon me as I depended upon her. Had she women to keep her company I would have gone.

So I went back to the game. It was fascinating in a way. I was quite good at it. I knew the symbols for all the numbers, and on one cold and stormy day with a norther blowing outside and a blizzard of snow making visibility less than the length of my arms, I mastered a concept which the eye had been pressing on me for a long time. I learned that the symbols did not halt and become senseless after reaching the number of fingers on two hands, but that the double slash mark meant ten and one and not two and that by adding a symbol after the slash mark denoting one, the value of the symbol became ten and two, ten and three and on up. Then, just as I felt smug at having mastered that part of the game, the eye came with a new concept which puzzled me. By the addition of a small symbol, $+$, between two symbols the numbers took on a new meaning, and when I learned, finally, that $2 + 2$ is 4, the game took on a complexity which bored Mar and left her playing with our babies while I spent more and more time sitting in the chair pushing symbols on the flat surface to get the eye to react.

Then the game was almost ruined when, without warning, the eye made a strange noise. I had been playing happily, using the + symbol and doing well, and suddenly the eye changed, a color glowed in it, and there appeared a picture on the eye much like a picture drawn by a child in the sand with a stick, the straight-line representation of a man with arms out-flung, five fingers on each hand. And as I mused and wondered what form the game was now taking, the eye made noise. I leaped back and could not make any sense out of the sound. It was strangely human but grating to my ears, low, full. I stayed away from the chair for a while, and then, hoping that the numbers game would be played, went back. The stick man ap-peared and the sound came. I pushed at the flat surface and nothing happened, and then I noticed that there was a series of pictures now on my flat surface. A man. A tree, other things, and under each picture there were little lines much like the symbols for numbers, but dif-ferent. And then there appeared on the eye the little lines under the picture of the man and the sound came again. I listened carefully. The sound repeated. I called Mar.

"Listen," I said.

"I do not like the game," she said.

"Just listen."

"Man, man, man"—the eye was making sound, in a deep, full, reasonating sound which was vaguely human but not like the pleasantly high voices of our people.

"It is saying 'man,' " I said. "And there is the pic-ture of a man."

I looked at the flat surface. The picture of the man was glowing, and I pushed it. The picture on the eye changed. There was a tree, and the deep voice was say-ing, " 'Tree, tree, tree.' " Yes, as my ears grew accus-tomed to it and my fright faded, it was speaking, the eye. I pushed the tree symbol, and a new game was born. There seemed to be an endless supply of pic-tures. Cloud. Rain. Bear. Tree. Stream. Woman. Child. And the voice of the eye repeated each endlessly until

I silenced it by pushing the picture on the flat surface, and after days of this, with winter clinging even though spring was near, the game changed slightly, going over the familiar pictures but not showing me the picture on the flat surface but, instead, giving me only the little symbols, which I concluded, meant the object just as the symbols could mean numbers.

I had trouble remembering, but the eye repeated and repeated, and then we were doing games like Man + Woman = Child. I liked the one which went Tree + Rain + Sun = Fruit.

As the days lengthened and the snow melted in our valley and the stream was swollen with the melt runoff, I deserted the game, save for periods at night, and watched my valley come to life. There was still snow on the heights, and the nights were quite chill. My son, Egan, named for my father, had shown signs of being ill. It was an illness for which I could see no reason. He ate well, taking milk from Mar's full breasts and, in addition, eating food which Mar chewed for him, but he was not growing as rapidly as Margan, the girl. And he cried often, a weak and protesting cry which tore at my heart, for nothing I could do, nothing I could bring down by my prayers, seemed to help him.

Thus, my journey into the range of man was delayed. Thinking that the food from the magic cave might not be good for my son, I hunted and Mar chewed freshly cooked meat for my son and fed him. There seemed to be a slight improvement, and so our lives went back to almost normal, except that we could not bring ourselves to desert the comforts of our cave, for as the days warmed, there was a pleasant coolness inside.

In the evenings I would play the game, and there was always something new. We started a new kind of game, the eye and I, and I laughed, for I knew more than the eye. The eye showed, in pictures like the pictures drawn in the sand by a child, how to make a

stone ax. I had made stone axes when I was a child, so
I laughed. Then the eye showed how to make a
longbow, one step at a time, and I nodded in agreement. How to make fire by the spinning stick and the
thong of leather? Ha. Any child knew that. But a
house built of logs? Very interesting. I saw immediately
the advantages of that. Thick walls to keep out the
cold. A roof formed of saplings and sod. Yes. I could
see that. I punched the symbol for the log house
again and again until I had the process learned, and I
practiced, cutting trees and notching them and putting
them together into a square. How much I could teach
my fellow men had I the chance.

I became interested in the eye's showing of how to
make pottery and was intrigued when the eye added
something new. By forming a small cave of stone and
chinking the holes with clay and building a fire inside
to burn to glowing embers, the clay pots were made
harder. I forced Mar to watch, and we tried, and the
pots we made were almost as hard as dragonskin and
much prettier than those which were hardened merely
by putting them into the embers of a campfire.

With so much knowledge, I was bursting to tell it. In
spite of Egan's continued weakness, we packed and left
our valley through the dragon hole. I was still unde-
cided. Mar favored a trip to the nearest range of a
family, there to try to form an alliance, but I kept
thinking of my home, of the Valley of Clean Waters,
and wondering if any of my old—friends—were alive.
And although it was far, I set my trail to the northeast-
ward.

To Mar's disgust, I kept our hair scraped. She
wailed and complained that the sun burned her bare
scalp, but I could see, as we began to encounter
families, that it was wise, for we were welcomed. I sub-
mitted my son to the eyes of the wise old women of
each family as we journeyed, had many prayers, fed

him many potions, but he was still weak and frail, while Margan seemed to thrive on travel.

I found man to be much the same everywhere in the mountains. Although a family would guard its range, there was no malice to strangers, such as we, and we were welcomed everywhere, especially as I began to become known as Eban the Teller of Tales. We dawdled away a summer going northward. Margan began to crawl. Poor Egan was runted and weak, wanting only to sleep on his mother's breast.

It was a Seer of the family of Welo the Wise who thought to submit the boy to her bare belly, there to feel the faint but unmistakable tingle of warning from deep within his bones.

"The boy has the sickness," the old woman said.

"How can that be?" I asked.

"You tell of your travels to the east," she said. "Perhaps you brought it."

"Would I not feel it in myself?" I asked. I wondered why I had not thought to test carefully both my children, and that night, in the privacy of a hidehouse furnished us as guests, I held both the children to my belly and to my sadness felt the warning tingle in both. However, the spirit was in Mar, and she lived. And Margan was as healthy as a little girl could be. It was not that. No, it was something else, and I knew not what.

It was with a heavy heart that I quickened our journey to the north and the east, and when at last I recognized landmarks, knowing the country in which I was born, the country from which Strabo of the Strongarm had led the family, I made long marches and crossed three ridges, and there, below, was the Lake of Clean Water and the hidehouses of a family nearby. I went into the valley with a mixture of emotions.

The young ones saw us coming and came out to meet us as we approached the hidehouse along the shore of the lake. They danced and sang and stared.

Women stood near their houses, watching our approach. I looked eagerly for a familiar face and saw an old woman who looked familiar. I went closer. They were making signs of welcome. A man came from a hidehouse, the place of the family head, and I recognized Logan, son of Logman. And then the old woman was speaking.

"Stranger, you are welcome."

"My thanks," I said. "We have come far."

She looked very familiar. "Are you not Bla the Window?" I asked.

She looked at me strangely. "I was once known by that name. I am, and have been for many moons now, the Seer of Things Unseen."

"Welcome," said Logan, son of Logman, coming up to us and looking at us with his head cocked. "Gods of man," he said.

"Yes, Logan," I said.

"It cannot be. The killbird got you, along with Strabo and the others."

"No, I fell beyond his death," I said.

Logan's face was grim. "Eban the Hunter," he said.

"Yes. I have done penace. I have traveled far, and the gods of man have seen fit to forgive and give me an opportunity to repay my debt to my people."

"How can that be?" Logan asked. "For you are the bringer of death."

"Honorable father," I said, giving him his due as family head, "did you not tempt the gods of man as I did?"

"You were chosen," he said. "And then you dived straight toward the dome where the family waited."

"I was merely exercising the right to take evasive action."

"I retract my words of welcome," Logan said. "Go from us, bringer of death."

"I ask a hearing, and I bring gifts," I said. I looked over Logan's shoulder, and there stood Yuree, more beautiful than I could remember, her body grown into adulthood, thick, short, desirable. She carried an infant on her hip.

"It is his right," said Bla the Window, now Seer of Things Unseen.

"So be it," Logan said.

Before the family, which had not, of course, had time to grow to its former size, I stood. I looked and saw the faces of Yorerie the Butcher and by his side a young woman who, when I left, had not been of age. There were Cree and Young Pallas and all of them, but half the family was missing, and the remaining ones looked glum and unhappy, and there were, in their bodies, in their faces, the looks of hunger and winter sickness.

"Speak, haired one," Logan said.

I drew a knife of dragonskin from my clothing where I had hidden it and presented it to Logan. "For you, honorable father," I said.

He examined it and reluctantly let the others hold it. There was much excitement. I saw that some of the younger males had stone axes. Had they looted the dragon which I had slain? From the stock which I had carried—I was rich in dragonskin, with the dragon of the hole to loot at will—I presented each male who had none the material from which to fashion a hardax.

"Now speaks Eban the Hunter," I said, when the gifts had been examined. "I have traveled far and I have prayed to the gods of man and they have told me to come, to share my good fortune with my people, for I have found a land of plenty, and there are dragons, some which I have slain, for looting, for hardax and other treasures. There is game so fat that a man can live well, and there is magic which I, Eban the Hunter, would share with my people to repay a little what I, in my youth, brought down upon the heads of my own family. I have suffered and I have paid penance, and now it is time for me to atone. I beg of you to come with me to this land of plenty and share with me and my pairmate the gifts of God."

"We be of the Valley of Clean Waters," Logan said.

"We have not always been of the Valley of Clean Waters," I said.

"Had we hunters enough, the game is gone," said Yorerie, his speech not much improved.

"In the land beyond the mountains to the south there are deer so numerous that a chance arrow slays," I said.

"The family of Logan, son of Logman, does not follow a haired one," Logan said.

"The family of Logan the son of Logman hungered during the winter," Yorerie said. "I, for one, will listen to the tales of Eban the Hunter."

I told of my land, of the sweet valley. I did not tell of the magic of our cave, but hinted that I had magic to feed a family in time of need or in the dead of winter. I could see that some were interested. Yorerie, for certain. Cree the Kite. Young Pallas was obviously tempted, but Logan's old running mate, Teetom, was sneering.

We ate. The fare was meager. "It was a young deer," Yorerie said, "small and of little meat, and I was lucky to find him."

I told them that we could, by leaving soon, arrive in my land of plenty with time to build, to set up camp before the snows.

"And we would be without food for the winter, with no time to hunt, to kill, to have the butcher do his work, to dry the meat," Logan said.

"We kill and dry along the way," I said. "And I have ample stores to feed all the family for the winter should we not accumulate enough."

"I hear promises," Logan said.

"You hear the word of Eban," I said. "For I have never lied."

"We will speak, each to his own," Logan said. "Teetom, how say you?"

"I stay," Teetom said, with a scowl at me.

"Cree?"

"I would hear more."

"Yorerie?"

"I will go with the Hunter," Yorerie said.

"You will do as the family decides," Logan said. And he went around the fire. Young Pallas would go. But of all the rest of the sadly diminished family, no one spoke in my favor.

"So be it," Logan said. "All but Yorerie and Young Pallas vote to stay in our homeland, in the Valley of Clean Water. Thus, we all stay."

"I beg to have a hearing and a decision by the elders," Yorerie said, "for that is my right. Every man has the right to leave and start his own family."

"Every man has a duty to his family," Logan said, "and you are the last of the Butchers. I ask the elders to consider this and order you to stay and do your duty."

"I, too, would have a hearing," Young Pallas said.

"The family's in great need of hunters," Logan said. "To lose one hunter is more than the family can bear, since many of our great hunters were slain by the killbird which Eban the Hunter brought down to us."

The elders withdrew from the group around the fire and talked among themselves. The new Seer was the spokesman. "It is sad," she said, "to take a man's freedom which is his right by custom, but the family head is right. To lose the strong arm of Young Pallas and the skills of Yorerie would not be in the best interest of the family."

I stood. "I beg you," I said. "I did not come to plant the seeds of division among my family but to lead all to a land of ease and plenty. Logan, I offer you my services. I am no mean hunter. Come with me. All of you. You will see."

"If you are willing to serve, you may build a hide-house near us—"

"But not as a member of the family?" I asked, my face burning.

"And earn your way back into the family by serving," Logan said.

"Not even a great hunter could serve well in this place," I said, "for it is as Yorerie says. The game is hunted out, as is often the case when a family stays in one place too long. You will have to move on soon, so why not follow me to the best hunting range of all the mountains?"

"It is for the family head to decide when it is time to move a family," Logan said firmly. "And I say that the game is not hunted out, that the Valley of Clean Waters is our home."

"So be it, then," I said. "I will seek elsewhere, among the families to the south, who will listen and who will follow me to the land of plenty. I grieve for you."

There was only one more incident before we withdrew from the family to camp far away along the lake. I went to Yuree and, prostrating myself at her feet, said, "Yuree, honorable mother I beg, before I leave forever to have your forgiveness."

She took a long time to answer. I looked up. She was weeping silently.

She spoke at last. "If it were only me I would forgive, and gladly. You were the bravest of the brave, Eban, and you did not willingly bring death to my father and mother and the others, but . . ."

"Cannot you say it? I care not for the others now. But I would like your blessing, your forgiveness."

"I cannot," she said.

"So be it," I said.

We slept apart and traveled with the sun, leaving as we had come, alone, just our little group of four. Now we were both eager to be back in our sweet valley as soon as possible, so we did not dawdle, and thus it was several days before I heard, as we made camp, the sound of approach and a voice crying, "Ho, the camp-fire."

"Come near, friend," I said, standing with my long-bow at the ready, expecting to see a stranger, for we were crossing the range of a family with whom we had visited on the trip to the north. Instead it was Yorerie the Butcher who came into the glow of my fire.

"Ha, Eban, you travel swiftly," he panted.

"Welcome, Yorerie, my friend," I said. "What brings you?"

"I have exercised my freedom," he said. "My pair-mate and my child are on the trail behind us, along with the group of Cree the Kite. We will join you, Eban, if you will still have us."

"Gladly," I said. "But did the elders reconsider their decision?"

"No," he said, looking somewhat shamed.

"To go against the wishes of the family is a serious matter," I said. "Have you considered the whole of it? You can never go back, Yorerie."

"Logan is a bad family head," Yorerie said. "He takes the best portions of the meat for himself, unlike the old days when Strabo the Strongarm shared and shared alike with the entire family. And he is lazy and frightened, scared to move the family to new range lest he be wrong and be challenged for his position by one of the men in the family."

I was saddened to see my family, what was left of it, punished further because of me. Better if I had stayed in my valley. And yet there were Yorerie and Cree and their pairmates and children to consider, for life was obviously not good in the Valley of Clean Waters. I made my decision.

"You and all the others are welcome and will have my support and help," I said.

We slept, and on the morning I went back along the

trail and, after a full day's march, found the small
group trudging along. They were heavily laden, even
the young ones, the oldest of which could scarce walk,
carrying a share. And in addition to Cree the Kite, his
pairmate and his two children, there were two others.

"Seer," I said, bowing to the woman who had become the Seer of Things Unseen, "it is a surprise."

"I ask your blessings," the Seer said. "And for my
daughter." She motioned, and a tall, thin girl well past
the coming of age came forward, her thin shoulders
bowed under a heavy pack. "My daughter, Ouree,"
Seer said. "It is because of her that I desert my family
and cast my fortunes with you, Eban the Hunter, for
the stars and the ashes of the ceremonial fire have spoken to me and they say that Eban is a man of
greatness and generosity and will help my daughter."

"Your words make me blush," I said. "I will do all
that I can. What is it you wish?"

"For you to erase the shame which came to us, my
daughter and myself, when she came of age and no
preman spoke for her," Seer said sadly.

"That is a problem," I said, "for in my land there
are no men."

"You have a son," Seer said. "Yorerie has a son.
They will come of age. I ask only that when they do,
one of them, at the pleasure of the family head, give
Ouree a child to comfort her in her last years."

"So be it," I said. It is a thing which I had never
seen, the temporary pairing of an unclaimed woman
solely for the purpose of giving child, and I was
shamed for both Seer and for the girl, Ouree. And,
indeed, I did not understand why she had gone unclaimed. True, she was not beautiful. She was, I realized with a shock, much like me, without the short,
thick and beautiful limbs of the people. But she was
strong, as witness the load she bore without complaint.

I led them, slowly because of the young ones and
the women, to join my pairmate and Yorerie, who

rested after his run to catch us, and then we traveled as a group, and it was good, so good. Yorerie and Cree were good hunters. As the new family unit marched, they went into the hills and returned with game, and thus our carry loads increased with the hides of the deer and our pace was slowed.

We were thirteen—three hunters, two pairmates, five children, the Seer and her unclaimed daughter. Of the children, two were boys. My Egan and Yorerie's boy, named Boulee. Three hunters to provide for ten others. But in my range it would be easy, especially with our magic cave of the food. I had no worries and, in fact, was happier than I'd ever been, for there was no close blood claim between the families of Cree, Yorerie and myself, so mating could be accomplished among our children.

We reached our home without incident, and before we entered the valley through the dragon hole I carefully showed Yorerie and Cree the dangers of the dragons of the hilltops, warning them never to make approach to the valley save through the dragon hole. I took them all into my valley, discarding my former plans to place them outside the valley in the unclaimed and rich range there. Mar, who had been doubtful at first, was happy, too, and became great friends with the females, especially the unclaimed Ouree.

The first few days were spent in hunting. Then I led Cree and Yorerie in the making of log houses, after the instructions of my magic eye. They were astounded. I told them I had seen log houses in my travels, not willing as yet to share my magic, knowing the superstitions of my people. I feared that they would consider my magic tainted and turn against me.

It was but the work of a half moon to build housing for the family, three houses of logs on high ground near the creek and outside the marshy growth which hid our magic cave. Our days were spent together, and at night Mar and I left them to their houses to retreat to our cool cave.

One night after the log houses were finished and meat was drying in the sun and the women were working hides to warm them during the coming winter, Yorerie the Butcher reminded us that it was time for the rite of the changing year, the family celebration of the end of summer and the beginning of the time of colored leaves. With Seer of Things Unseen at her post on the hollowed logdrum, the females danced. I could not help but notice that Ouree the Unclaimed was unusually graceful. Indeed, Ouree was, in my opinion, a rare and valuable female, for she worked harder than any of us and, to the amusement of Yorerie and Cree, fashioned a longbow for herself and spent long hours in practice until, in the last of summer, she went forth alone and came home, a deer carcass dwarfing her as it was slung over her shoulders. In addition, she was our best cook, our best fashioner of hide garments, a tireless chewer of skin to prepare it, always willing to relieve one of the mothers of the care of the young. She was wonderful with our poor Egan, who walked now, but weakly, tiring quickly.

It was Yorerie who put a part of my thoughts into words that night of the end of summer rites when he leaned close and said, "We were all blind, Eban, to let that one go unclaimed."

"She is different," I said.

"As you are," he said. "But look how she sways. Look how gracefully she dances."

"I see," I said. I grinned at him. "I do see, my friend."

When the dancing ended, it was the Seer who spoke. "We have been led into a land of plenty," she said. "We have been shown new and wonderful things. We have homes which are warmer and stouter than the hidehouses, and we owe it to one man, to Eban the Hunter."

Cree the Kite stood. "We have spoken, the rest of us, in your absence, Eban the Hunter, and it is our wish that you serve us as family head."

"Ha, Eban," Yorerie said.

"I am honored," I said. "But we are as one, are we not? Why do we need a family head? Later, perhaps, when our family is large. In the meantime, we have the wisdom of the Seer to guide us in traditional things, and we work equally."

"Honorable father," Cree said, "my pairmate is with child. You cannot help but notice." We all laughed, for Roden, mate of Cree, was, indeed, far with child, her belly round and plump.

"I notice it now and then when he kicks," Roden said.

"Who, then, will bless my child when it is born?" Cree asked.

I nodded. A child needed the blessing of a family head, true. Still, I was selfish. I wanted to live in my cozy cave and have the companionship of my family when I wanted it. However, I could see my duty. "Would it be good if I suggested either Cree the Kite or Yorerie the Butcher for the honor?"

"You honor us," Yorerie said, "but we have spoken. Honor us truly, Eban."

"I honor you," I sighed, "as I am honored."

"Honorable father," they all said, and then we danced until the moon was low and the fires burned to embers.

I was happy.

And then the dragons spoke, on a chill end of summer morning.

7

We were gathered as a family that morning. The sun was over the hills trying to dispel the night's chill, and the skies were blue and we ate of the ripe nuts and the dried fruit of the harvest from the wild trees and lazed about, a family well prepared for the winter. The sound of the dragon spitting came. A short burst of sound which set my hair to rise, and then, a bit later, more, and then a whole chaos of sound as half a dozen of the dragons to the north of the dragon hole began to spit.

At first, when one dragon spoke, I thought of a poor unfortunate deer having wandered into the range of one of the hill dragons. Then with the others, so many of them, I felt a cold chill of dread.

"Yorerie, Cree," I said. "We go."

I led them at a trot to the dragon's hole and through, and then, having moved past the dead dragon of the hole out of range of the hill dragons, northward toward the point of the spitting sounds, which had long since died. My heart stopped when we heard, from a hollow between two ridges ahead, the wails of women in mourning.

You see, I knew, as surely as I was Eban the Hunter, I knew. None of the families in the south would have been so foolhardy as to walk into the face of the hill dragons. I knew, and when we topped a ridge and saw the people gathered below I recognized, first, the form of Yuree.

We ran down the hill recklessly, I tumbling and rolling to fetch up against a tree. Then, head ringing, I ran into the clearing beside a stream where the family was camped and saw Logan lying in his gore, on a blooded skin, his chest heaving, his blood still oozing from wounds on his chest and arms.

Three old men, several windows, children, the pairmates of the few remaining hunters of my old family, all wailed and mourned as Yuree knelt beside Logan.

Logan had led them directly into the teeth of the dragons.

I ran to kneel beside Yuree, full of remorse. Why had I not stayed with them? Why had I not insisted on leading them?

"Why did you change your mind, Logan?" I wailed. "Why did you lead them into the teeth?"

But he was far gone. I watched him die, his blood pumping out of a torn artery.

"How many?" I asked.

"All of the hunters," Yuree said, looking at me with cold eyes.

"Oh, God," I prayed. "Why me? Why do you choose me to continue to bring death to my own family?"

Yorerie put his hand on my shoulder. "Honorable father," he said. "It is not your fault."

"It is mine," I said. "I told him of the place of plenty, and they came at my invitation."

"No" Yorerie said pointing. I followed his finger and at Logan's blooded neck I saw the claws of war. I had never seen them before and there was a certain irony in it, since, in all probability, the bear claws which Logan wore to proclaim his intentions were probably from the bears killed by me or by my father. For never in the memory of the living had a tribe donned the bear claws and gone in search of an enemy with intent to kill. So precious was life that the last war between families had taken place in my father's father's lifetime.

"No," I said. "It cannot be."

An old man came forward. He prostrated himself at my feet. "We are yours, honorable father," he said, tears in his eyes.

"No, no, you are my family."

"Logan led a war party," Yorerie said, pointing to the bear claws. "Have them explain."

"Yes, please," I said, looking at Yuree. She had a sullen look on her face and would not meet my eyes.

"Old man," I said, "why did Logan come in war?"

"Because you stole the hunters Yorerie and Cree," the old man said. "Because you brought death to the family in the killbird and then took two of our few remaining hunters and left us to starve during the winter."

"And now all the hunters are dead," I said. "Even some of the old men. Are only these left, then?"

"We have not gone forward," the old man said. "For we fear the dragons. But from a distance I see bodies lying on the slopes. Only Logan crawled back."

"Fools," I said. "Oh, fools. And now what are we to do?"

"By the rules of the people they have warred on you," Cree said. "They are now your slaves."

"Slaves?" I wept. "They are my people."

"No longer," Yorerie said. "They have sworn to kill you and your family and to take what was yours." He sighed. "You are bound by the customs."

"I will not enslave my own," I said. "I give you your freedom. Go, what is left of you. Go and leave us in peace."

"Without hunters we will surely die," the old man said.

"True," Cree said.

"Then there is but one answer," I said, suffering,

wondering how many more punishments the gods of man had in store for me. "You will become of us."

Yuree looked at me, her eyes blazing. "Never," she spat. "Killer of my mother and father, killer of my pairmate, I will never join you."

"Logan's death and the death of the hunters is on his own head," Cree said heatedly.

"You others," I said, standing looking around at the mourning people. "Will you come into my valley? We will share. There is game for the taking. Will you come?"

"Gladly," said the old man, and all of the older ones agreed. Only two of the young windows who had so recently lost pairmates demurred, along with Yuree.

"So be it," I said. "But Eban the Hunter will not leave windows and children to starve in the cold of winter, and so I command you, Yuree, and all the others, to come. Come in freedom or come as slaves."

With a cry, Yuree launched herself at me, the sharp knife of dragonskin seeking my chest. I caught her arm. I had given the knife to Logan, and now his pairmate used it to try to kill me. I wrenched the knife away. "Tie her hands," I said. "And the others."

People leaped to obey me, their loyalties changing swiftly.

It was soon obvious to me that Yuree and the other two would be troublesome. We took all of the remaining members of my old family into the valley, where we men began to work to make log houses for the winter. There was food in plenty, and it was not too late to hunt. We fed them well and then considered the problem of Yuree and the two others, who tried, the first night, to escape.

"Honorable father," said Ouree the Unclaimed, "our men are few and are needed. And yet the slaves must be managed. May I offer myself?"

"A thankless job, Ouree," I said, "but it is yours, and my thanks to you. Treat them kindly. Perhaps they will relent, and should they do so, they can become of us."

And thus the unclaimed one spent her days managing the three slaves, slaves by choice, seeing to it that they did their share of work, guarding them against escape, for she was free, under the customs, to use the longbow which she had learned to wield so well should one of the slaves try to escape or offer threat to any member of the family. At first they were resentful, Yuree most of all, but gradually, as we treated them kindly, the other two relented and, with bodies flat to the ground, begged me, as family head, to release them from slavery. They promised to be good family members, and I granted it, and they took their place, sharing a log house between them with their several young ones. Only Yuree remained a slave.

We had serious problems. Logan the Unwise, as he had come to be called after his death, had even armed the premen nearing coming of age and had led them to their deaths, moving as a body directly into an area where several dragons could spit at once. The family's males were decimated, leaving only boys. Three old men beyond the age of mating, half a dozen old women, seven windows, counting Yuree, an even dozen children.

Three hunters—myself, Yorerie, Cree.

And yet there was plenty, and the family was settled in well when the snows came and I, at last, could find some peace in my cave with Mar and our two children. I went back to my game. There was a name for it, I found. The voice of the eye called it a word and the symbols were four. The game was called read. I read symbols for many things. I read about a man, a woman and a child building a log house. They were happy. I read many things. I read about the deer and the bear and things I did not understand, and I got the idea as the winter began to close in that I was reading about a race of giants, for the pictures on the eye were becoming more and more clear and the size of the chair in which I sat was like that of the chair things and couch things in the house of the giants far to the east, and I had much to wonder about.

On evenings I sometimes joined the family, there to tell tales. I told them about a race of giants who lived on our land in the time of the first dragons, and they were awed and interested. I told them of the travels of Eban the Hunter and his pairmate, of the sick and starving inbreeders of the low slopes, the monsters of the east.

And things were good. Only two things concerned me. One, of deadly concern, was the health of our child, Egan. He was pale and weak, and there were times when, as he learned to speak words, he would cry and say, "It hurts, it hurts," and rub his tiny little limbs with a look of pain so intense that I hurt as well. The second was Yuree, who continued to be a slave under the management of Ouree the Unclaimed. Both problems were to come to a crisis during that winter.

Egan worsened. He had no urge for food. We forced him to eat but he did not gain weight or grow. Our girl was fat and healthy and always moving with that endless energy of the very young. Poor Egan lay on his couch and cried with his pain. Before the shortest night of the year, he was in constant pain, and finally, a mere bag of bones, white as if all his blood had left him, he died in great pain and left his father and his mother to grieve. My poor son. My only son.

The family ate a feast of mourning, and we dug though snow and chipped away at frozen ground to place my Egan in his grave.

"I will retire for a period of mourning," I told the gathered family. "In my absence it is Yorerie to whom you will come, with the Seer as his adviser."

And for days I did not leave our cave. The only joy in my life was my daughter and my pairmate, and we clung to each other, the antics of the little girl sometimes making us forget, for a moment, our grief.

My own grief was compounded by Mar's failure to get with child. Cree's pairmate had delivered a fine son, and I envied him so.

I spent much time playing read, learning stories of the giants. Pictures showed giants riding animals of a strange form, four legs, long necks. There were no such animals in our land. It was a puzzle. And I longed to know more, spending more and more time at the game until, one night when both Mar and Margan were sleeping, the eye spoke to me.

"You are man," said the low and strange voice of the eye. I had come to understand it.

"I am man," I said in my pleasingly high voice.

"Man learns," the voice said.

"I learn," I agreed. Could the eye hear me? Yes, I thought so, for some of the games included voice. I could not make a picture change until I spoke the words desired by the eye.

"Man has duty to man," the eye said.

"Man has his duty," I agreed, nodding my head vigorously.

"And now it is time for your duty to begin," the eye said. "You are ready."

And before me the eye moved, an entire plate moving, sliding, opening a hole in the wall of the eye cave, and, curious, I looked to see step stones leading downward into a sunlit long cave which went down and down—I went without waking Mar—into a large and heated and sunlit cave which, at the center, had a chair and a tall thing of lights and other wonders. I walked near and examined. The tall thing extended to the top of the cave and was alive with lights, which, as I watched, began to blink in a pattern that was interesting. I took my place in the chair, and the flat surface in front of me came alive. It was, I discovered, another form of the game.

"Man," said the voice of the eye. "Now learn."

"I learn," I said.

A light came on on the tall part. I looked at my flat surface and saw a light. I pushed. There was a click and another light came on and there was a wait after I pushed the light which matched it and on my flat surface there were protruding things. I played the game until I was tired and left it to sleep.

The new game was more complicated than anything I had done and required an exactness which sometimes bored me. Often there was a waiting period as I pushed lights and protrusions and moved little things from one position to the other. When I made a mistake the tall thing lit up and made a sound like a lion wailing. Then the game had to be begun all over again.

After days of this I was bored, for there were no pictures.

"I will go back to the other game," I said, "the read game."

But the eye was not alive, and each time I entered the small cave of the eye the plate opened and there was nothing to do but go into the lower cave and push lights and move little things which clicked. I tired.

"Man has duty," the voice told me.

"I am tired of this."

"Man has duty. Man must do duty. Man will be rewarded with good things to eat and other wonders."

This was new. I listened. It was repeated. I followed the lights and pushed things and after a long day of it the voice said, "It is good. You are ready."

"I sleep," I said. "I am ready for that."

But there was not to be sleep. It was early evening, and when I went into the sleep cave above Yorerie was there, looking uneasy as he always did when he was in our cave. I had allowed him to visit us only after I had named him acting family head during my period of mourning. He did not like our cave.

"Honorable father," he said. "There is a problem."

"You are family head. If you need advice, ask the Seer."

"The Seer advised me to come to you, honorable father."

"Speak, then," I said. "I suppose it is time I ended my mourning."

"It is the young windows," Yorerie said. "They have spoken with the Seer of Things Unseen and they claim the right of family disaster."

"You will have to tell me," I said. "I am not as wise as the Seer and do not know all about our ancient customs."

"Indeed, the Seer herself had to search her memory, for she had never experienced disaster," Yorerie said.

"Speak," I told him.

"When disaster, as in war or disease, strikes the men of a family, leaving many windows, it is the right of the windows under our ancient laws to use the remaining hunters for the purpose of getting with child, thus to rebuild the strength of the family."

"Gods of man," I sighed. "Are we to become like the inbreeders?"

"Seer tells me it is true," Yorerie said.

"Sensible, if you ask me," said my Mar.

"Would you lend me, then, to the windows to make babies?" I asked her in amazement.

"Would you cease to love me if you did?" she asked. "Would it change you? Would you still not be Eban the Hunter?"

"Gods of man," I said.

I resolved to speak with the family. I gathered them on a clear and starry night before a huge and ceremonial campfire.

"I will hear the thoughts of all," I said. "Seer of Things Unseen, tell us the law."

"The family needs hunters," Seer said. "For soon all will be old and there are only five young ones who are male and they will have to feed and protect all. It is the right of windows, when males number fewer than females, to be serviced for the purpose of making child. So says the law. So says the Seer, for this family has, indeed, come to disaster."

"And the dangers?" I asked. "Are the laws of blood then repealed in time of disaster?"

"I have made a study," the Seer said. "The law, as I can remember it . . ."

Would that we had all our laws written on the eye, I thought to myself, there to be permanent and not to be trusted to the frail memory of a Seer.

". . . allows no coupling of sister and brother, parent and child, nor the coupling of sons and daughters of brothers and sisters. Thus, Cree the Kite would be banned from servicing two windows, who are daughters of his mother and father's sisters and brothers, Yorerie of two. Of the family, you alone, Eban, are not so close by blood, your father having no brothers or sisters and your mother coming from another family by capture. Since there are but three hunters, thus, you service the windows not serviceable by Cree and Yorerie."

"Gods of man," I said.

"We beg our rights," said one of the windows, prostrating herself in the cleared area beside the campfire.

"Arise," I said. "And how say the pairmates of Yorerie and Cree?" I asked.

Roden, pairmate of Cree, stood. "We like it not," she said, "but we abide by the law, provided that it is over when the windows are with child."

"That is the law," the Seer said. "When the windows are with child the family returns to normal until the new children are walkers, and then—"

"Again?" I asked, awed by the idea of fathering so many children.

"Until the balance is repaired and the boys of the family begin to reach age," the Seer said.

"This is for the family," I said. "A vote."

The windows voted, save Yuree, who was silent. The old voted and then the pairmates, Mar grinning at me with mischief in her eyes. That left only the hunters. Yorerie, clearly red-faced, said he would do his duty, his eyes on the pleasing form of one of his appointed windows. Cree said yes.

"So be it," said I.

"Honorable father," Yuree the Slave said, prostrating herself.

"You may speak," I said.

"I beg forgiveness," she said. "If it is still your will to give me another chance to be a member of your family, I beg your blessing."

"Gladly," I said. "Slave Yuree, arise." She stood. "Welcome, sister," I said. "As family head, I make Yuree the Window a member, and all are to treat her as such."

"Honorable father," Yuree said, a little smile on her face. "Am I not a full member?"

"I have granted it."

"I claim my right," she said.

"As a family member you have all rights," I said.

"Both Yorerie and Cree are sons of sisters of my mother," Yuree said, with that funny little smile. I realized the import and looked quickly at Mar. She was no longer smiling.

"The family has spoken," I said. "So be it."

"Honorable father," the Seer of Things Unseen said, "here are the windows to be honored by your seed. Young Til, who was childless, having only this summer come of age; Fanan the window of Bloc; now that she is no longer a slave, Yuree window of Logan; and, lastly, the daughter of Bla, Ouree the Unclaimed."

"Does the Unclaimed have the right of disaster?"

"Clearly," the Seer said.

"So be it," I muttered, looking at Yuree with a strange feeling of anticipation surging in my blood.

Thus it was that the winter passed. I will not speak

much of the events, for such things are private and, except in times of disaster, kept within the hidehouse of pairmates. Let me say only that Young Til was shy and sent me away quickly when my duty was done, she being the first of my duties, the times chosen by the moon as interpreted by the Seer, and that Fanan was easily pleased, begged me to stay—I did, on two occasions until the sun was a redness, Fanan pleasing as well as being pleased; and that Ouree the Unclaimed was so grateful for my attentions that it made me feel ashamed. I found her to be untouched, of course, and it was the work of two nights to penetrate her tightness, and then she was tender, loving, grateful, and brought gifts of pretty red berries to Mar to thank her for allowing me to present her with child, for she was the first to miss her moon period.

It was Yuree who was a puzzle. I went into her house with sinful anticipation, feeling very much as if I had, in my mind, joined the honorless inbreeders, to be so able to find joy in thinking of coupling with her. She was ready for me, allowed no preliminary play, but guided me to her quickly and was quickly done with me. However, of the four to whom I gave service, she was the last to miss her moon period, and thus after all the other three were finished with me I was still visiting the house of Yuree after two winter moons, much to Mar's disgust.

So. It was, I must admit, an interesting winter, one which saw me out of my cave many nights, leaving me no time for the game. When I went back to it, having only Yuree left to service, I was slow to follow the lights, and we had to begin all over again.

In view of later events I must depart from my honor and speak of my last night with Yuree. I went to her house, as was my duty, prepared for a joyless coupling quickly done and quickly finished, wondering if I was fated to spend my virile years servicing two women who could not, apparently, conceive. She awaited me. The fire was stacked with green wood, the house was warm, and she was in her couch, covered by her sleephides. I removed my clothing and joined her. I lay beside her, not speaking, waiting for the heat of her desirable body to prepare me. She touched me. It was something she had not done before. Her hand was warm and soft, and I responded immediately and started to mount her, to do my duty quickly. She would not open for me; instead, she began to use her lips on mine, to cling and love as the others had loved, and as she had not done. And it was good. I allowed her.

"There is a change," I sighed, as she kissed and clung and fondled.

"That is because this is the last night," she said.

"How can you say?"

"I know. I feel it," she said. "Tonight I will conceive, and your duty will be finished, and I wish to make it memorable."

"Yes," I said. For foolish moments I dreamed that the killbird had slept, leaving me to win Yuree, and that this was our first time and I was warm, and then I felt a pang of disloyalty.

"I want to show you, Eban, what a woman can be," she whispered, and continued to do things to me until, with a roar of need, I mounted her and she was alive and responsive and loving, and then it was ended.

"Was it good?" she whispered.

"Very good," I said.

"I wanted it to be good, so that you would remember," she said.

"There will be other times," I said. "When your child is a walker there will be other times."

"No," she said. "You will never touch me again."

There was something in her voice. I withdrew my slackness from her and cleaned myself, wondering.

"But," she said, "when you are with your skinny and ugly hag of an inbreeder, you will remember and lust for Yuree."

So much malice? I was stunned. But I spoke. "Mar is neither skinny nor ugly," I said. "She is my pairmate by choice, Yuree. And although you were sweet, until this malice which I did not suspect came out in you, you are not the woman Mar is, for she knows delights which you have not imagined."

Her face darkened.

"The art of love is hers," I said, "and she uses her lips and her hot tongue in such ways as to make other women seem passive. So, Yuree, you have not hurt me. I will not lust for you."

"Killer," she spat. "Know, then, that I have already missed my moon period and am with your child and that it is so for one reason and one alone. I will bear a boy. He will live and grow to kill you, killer, and be family head."

"Yuree, your hate has poisoned you. If it be a son, he will be a family member and have as much chance to win family head as the others. But do not poison his mind against me or I will try you for disloyalty."

"I hate you," she said. "I'm glad your sickly infant son died."

I struck her across the face heavily, sending her head back against the couch, and then I left her to her own hate, much disturbed.

8

During our long periods of being alone, having no one in the world save ourselves, Mar and I had developed the habit of sharing every thought. Indeed, she questioned me closely when I returned from each of my duty periods with the four women I serviced and often laughed at my accounts. After my last visit to Yuree I was troubled and waited a day to speak with Mar.

"The sickness of hate is in her," Mar said. "Perhaps a child will change it.'"

"She has right to hate me," I said. "For I brought death to father, mother, family, pairmate."

"I'm sick of your blaming yourself for all of that," Mar said. "'Think of the good you've done for these people. Look at the love which is given you, with honor, by all save the soured one. Do you actually think she hates you?"

"Are you saying she doesn't, when she told me she did, and promised to rear her son to kill me?"

"She loved you, fool," Mar said. "She has always loved you. She sent you to get the dragon guts. But she loved you. She thought you dead and took a weak man, and this has soured her, for she sees you with me and thinks it is her right to be at your side in your sleep couch."

"Wrong, wrong," I said. "She hates me because of the death I brought into her life."

"Ha," Mar said. "Go to her, then, tell her you are

tired of the inbreeder and will be her pairmate, and see how quickly her frown changes."

"Mar," I said, shocked.

"Oh, I know you wouldn't," she said. "You're much too honorable. But it is true, what I speak."

"Mar, have you ever doubted my love for you?"

She smiled, came to me, pushed me back and put her sweet weight atop me. "Never," she said. "My only regret is that I cannot give you babies."

"We have Margan."

"With the sickness, as you tell me, in her bones. Promise me one thing, Eban."

"Of course."

"Keep that our secret."

"The sickness?"

"Yes."

"So be it."

"You will have children. Sons and daughters by all of them. The four."

"They will not be ours, but theirs."

"No," she said. "We will make them ours, even the offspring of Yuree. You are family head. You can speak. You can demand the right of the father."

"All would give it gladly, save Yuree."

"And you will force it on her, or you will raise the thing you fear, a killer, in your bosom," Mar said.

"You are wise, as always," I said.

So we watched with interest as the spring came and a summer of joy began, the family happy, well fed, eager, industrious, together. Even Yuree seemed resigned. Bellies fattened with summer. We had come to share food, especially the sweets which came from our magic cave, with all. Huge and noisy gatherings took place in front of our cave, and Mar served the sweets and all grew fat and the looted wealth from the dragon of the hole kept us in arrow heads and hard axes.

Rich in food, clad in the finest skins, swimmers for

the harvesting, fruit on the trees, we prospered and swam together in the cool waters of the stream, and we hunters began to teach the boys and the women taught the females and suddenly summer was over and bellies were huge, all seven of the windows with child and all to be delivered within two moons. The time of the color of leaves came, and young Til was the first of my windows to birth, a girl. Now the village was a place of groans and scurrying women as child after child was born, not only to the seven windows but to the pair-mates of Yorerie and Cree. Fanan give birth to a boy. Ouree the Unclaimed presented the family with a fine girl. Yuree, the last, birthed a girl.

Ouree was weak, after the birth, and Mar moved her into our cave so that she could tend child and mother. Ouree was so gentle, so eager to please. She recovered, and the little girl was fat and healthy, sucking milk from Ouree with an eagerness which set us all laughing. Our daughter, Margan, fell in love with the baby. When Ouree was recovered and made preparation to move into her own house, Margan cried and protested.

"Come stay with me, then," Ouree said.

"You stay us," Margan lisped.

"Why not?" Mar asked. "You are welcome. There is room."

"But you are pairmates and need your privacy," Ouree said.

"When we want privacy we will go into the cave of the games below," Mar said. "Stay. Your daughter is our daughter, and our house is your house."

She stayed.

I saw Yuree, baby on back, as I walked along the stream.

"Why does the Unclaimed one live with you?" Yuree asked without greeting.

"She and Mar are friends," I said.

"And she, being skinny and ugly like the inbreeder, appeals to you. Do you service them both at once?"

"You have the tongue of an evil demon," I said.

"You failed me," Yuree said.

"How?"

"It is a girl," she said, speaking of her baby.

"A very pretty little girl. She will have her mother's eyes and body."

"Eban . . ."

"Yes, Yuree."

"A blessing."

"Gladly."

"Come lie with me. Make me with child now. I must have a son to care for me in my old age."

"I was never to touch you again," I said, unable to resist.

"I was angry. Come. I will make it nice for you."

"You know the custom," I said. "Only when the baby walks."

"God curse the custom," she said.

It was only nights later when the women heard a wail from Yuree's tent and ran to find her holding the lifeless baby. When I arrived the women were already wailing.

"It is God's curse," Yuree said. "The baby died in her sleep."

My little girl. I had not known her, for Yuree had not even presented her for my inspection, and I was too concerned about Yuree's feelings to go to her. I grieved, inside, and walked away to let the women mourn and prepare the small body for burial. The Seer of Things Unseen caught me, took my arm.

"I must speak," she said. I nodded. "God did not come in the night," she said. "The baby was smothered in her own bed, by her own sleepskins."

"How can this be?"

"Ask Yuree," she said. "Only a careless mother allows her baby to smother. Careless, or . . ."

"Can you even suggest it?" I asked, shocked.

"She wanted a boy. Already, even as you walked out

the door, while she should have been mourning, she told me she demanded the right of the window, and that means you to service her, now."

"If it is her right—"

"But what did she do to earn that right before the baby walked?" Seer asked.

"Seer," I said, "you are a wise woman, but you are wrong. I have never told this. Only Mar knows. But in defense of my own life I have taken life, inbreeder life, and it is a horrible and saddening thing. No. You must not suggest it. Carelessness? Perhaps. Intent? No mother could do such."

"Women have done strange things for love," Seer said. "And Yuree has had more than her share of grief. Perhaps it has sickened her mind."

"No, no," I said. I could not even think it. But, gods of man, how many times I have wished that I had listened to the old Seer that night of the death of Yuree's girl baby.

I went to Yuree's house to do my duty, and she wept and clung to me and begged me to stay the night, which I did, and then other nights, as the Seer decreed, judging Yuree's fertile period by the moon, and I, myself, took note of the time of Yuree's blooding, and when, going there on her request, I knew that she was not blooding at the time, I said to her, "Yuree, if you are missing your moon period my duty is finished."

"I confess," she said. "I am missing it, but I am not sure. A few more nights to make certain, Eban."

"I cannot. I will go."

"Eban, please, for me. I am so lonely. I want your body so."

"No, Yuree," I said. "A family head, of all people, must observe the customs."

"If you go I will kill myself," she said.

I went pale. "That is the sin of all sins," I said. "Do not speak such evil."

"Go, then," she said. "I hope you enjoy your rutting with your inbreeder."

Man, I suppose, is an imperfect creature and must live in an imperfect world. In my life there was only one unhappiness. Yuree. She was with child. Winter came. She would seek me out and beg me to come to her, to sneak into her house in the night. She said things like, "The inbreeder won't care."

Finally I had enough and I told her, "Yuree, I warn you, and it is a warning from the family head. Remember your honor. Observe our customs. Do your work and be happy or I will call the council of the entire family to punish you." I spoke sternly and thought the matter settled, for she ceased to seek me out.

Snow came, and the young were doing well. Ouree was like a member of our own family and her young one was a joy to me and to Mar. The two females fussed over the baby endlessly, aided by my daughter, Margan. I went back to my game, which was the same and boring, but I was getting some satisfaction out of doing it almost right every time.

The thing came suddenly. We watched Margan play with the baby one night. There was a knocking on the plate and I opened it. Yuree was there. She had a long-bow in her hands and a dragonskin arrow was in place, the bow stretched. It was pointed at me.

"I give you one last chance," Yuree said. "Leave them and come with me."

My impulse was to strike the bow from her hands, but there was a madness in her eyes. "Yuree," I said gently. "Put aside the bow. Come. We will talk. All of us."

"Yes or no, killer," she said. "Come with me or I will repay you in kind for the death you have given me."

"Yuree, Yuree," I said soothingly, moving forward, seeing that she was maddened. I would knock the bow aside and the arrow would fly, if she released it, into one of the hard walls, doing no damage, but she saw my intent and with a wild cry loosed the arrow, which made a zipping sound as it passed my very cheek, and a cry of pain came from behind me even as I hit Yuree with my closed hand and sent her sprawling into the snow. I turned then and screamed. Mar was on her knees, and the arrow, so wickedly tipped with jagged dragonskin, was lodged deeply in her breast. I screamed my rage and pain and leaped to catch her as she fell forward.

The arrow was deep. The head was jagged. And yet, it had to come out.

"Eban," she whispered. "Oh, Eban. Hold me."

"Yes, yes," I said. I held her. "We must remove the arrow."

"No," she said. "It hurts so."

"It must come out, and then we will fix it and you will be well again soon."

"No," she whispered. "Eban . . ." And the dull look of death came to her eyes, which had been so alive and so loving, and I sat there, rocking her as the last of her breath went in a shudder and her legs did a violent little dance, and Margan was screaming and Ouree weeping and the baby crying, and maddened Yuree came, dragonskin knife in hand, screaming.

My hardax is never far from my side and it was at my side, and with one arm supporting Mar's dead body I heaved the ax, and it took the killer in the stomach, burying itself. Yet still she came, the knife aimed at me. I rolled aside to dodge it and hit her with my closed hand, and she fell to the floor, bleeding, screaming now, and her blood mingled with Mar's and then she was dead.

Gods of man. Gods of man. You are cruel and evil and endlessly inventive in the miseries you can imagine to heap upon your creatures.

9

Eban the Accursed. Has any man ever had so much death? A man buries his parents when they die peacefully in their old age. Now and again a man sees death. A hunter misses the vital point and the bear reaches him. In my father's case death was distant, for he died by a dragon far from home, and his bones, I suppose, whiten on some hillside near a dragon's lair. My mother died slowly and quietly. And then it came. Blast of killbird. Slash of ax at the inbreeders. The sickness claiming my son. Rattle of dragon's teeth as more members of my family died. My child by Yuree, and, I came to suspect, at Yuree's hands, for she was mad. And me, once again dealing death with my ax, and to a woman whom I had once loved, a woman I had serviced, whose arms I had known, whose belly had fertilized my seed and developed it. Blood and death and—

Mar. Mar. Mar.

I drove Ouree away. Then I tossed Yuree's body into the snow and closed the plate. Margan, not really knowing what was going on, had been snatched up by Ouree, along with Ouree's own baby. I cradled Mar's body in my arms and sang the song of mourning until I fell into a stupor and woke, limbs stiff and crying done.

Outside, as I carried Mar's body, the family greeted me with a wail of mourning, and we sang the song of death and sadness as Mar joined the body of our unlucky son in the frozen ground.

141

I spoke to them.

"I am Eban the Sad, Eban the Accursed, Eban the Dead, for I live not from this day."

"Speak not so, honorable father," Ouree said, weeping.

"I mourn alone. Do not come to me. And hear this. From this day I banish death from our valley. I will not allow it near. I have had enough death. I have seen sacred life after sacred life ended before the appointed time. I will have no more of it. I will slay neither animal nor man, and I will eat only of the magic, for flesh, even if it is animal, is death."

Someone had entered my cave during the burial and washed away the blood of both Mar and the mad Yuree. I closed myself away. I ate nothing, drank only water. I became lightheaded. I went to the game cave, unable, since I had not been into the light outside, to know whether it was night or day, but I felt the passage of nights, how many I knew not. The game cave welcomed me with the usual display of lights, and I lost myself in following instructions, pushing and moving things until I was able to blank out everything from my mind but the flashing lights, the instructions of the deep and unnatural voice. How long? I know not. I pushed and thought of nothing and followed the instructions and hardly realized it when the voice said:

"Well done. You are ready."

And now still another plate opened, and there was a cave of wonders. I took the chair, very small in it, having to stand on my knees to see the flat surface with its things to push and move and the eyes were spread all across the thing in front of me, blank and white. However, they came to life, and I saw wonders which were a puzzle. Some eyes showed, gods of man it is true, killbirds. They sat, did the killbirds, on their tails and were dead or sleeping in caves of dragonskin.

The voice of the eye said strange things I did not understand. As best I can repeat the strangeness, it sounded like "See whence one." I pushed and moved and the eyes showed the killbirds and I wondered, but it was still a game. I was good at the game. I did not miss a move. Not once did the game make that wail like a dying lion and force me to begin again. It was a long game and there were times when, in a voice of deep and unnatural quality, I was told, "Hold." And in those times I sat and looked at the eyes and was amazed for they were constantly changing. There would be sort of a blink and the killbird shown there would be viewed from another angle. There was one eye which interested me more than the others. I know not what it was, for it was a fanciful thing. It was as if an eye had been taken aloft on the wings of man or a killbird and looked down from a height not attainable by man, even if he could fly without the danger of being punished by the gods of man. But it was not real, I knew, for the ever-extending earth, if man could see it from so great a height, up with the gods, would be as it is, flat, and this fanciful thing showed a falling away, and there were mountains below which were tiny and the entire scene was lovely, with white clouds drifting and the earth below green with a dot of blue showing now and then.

I know not how long I played the game, but it served to take my mind away from my unbearable sadness. And it was follow the lights and the voice and push and punch and wait and then I knew from our former games that we were nearing the end. Only a few more moves and then I would push down on a little thing which was as red as blood—and that thought put my mind back into its sadness and I almost failed to see the light which told me my next move. I mused about my edict banning death from my valley and I felt foolish, knowing how God laughed, for death comes to all things. However, I could abolish death in my own life. It came to me as a revelation. I could block the plate leading to the outside. There was food and water, and I could live the rest of my days in my cave, never seeing death, not so much as an insect, for there was something about the place which kept insects out. Ah, to know no more sorrow. But then a curiosity came. What of my children? My own Margan. Ouree's sweet little one. My sons and daughters by the other windows and my sons and daughters to come as I did my duty and serviced—and what of a pairmate? Oh, Mar. Mar. I will never have another. No one could replace you, my loved one, my all, my Mar.

Yes, I would have to go out. I would be family head. I would tell the evil of death and, in times of plenty, I would journey into the ranges of other families and make alliances and preach the evils of death, which in violent form save from dragons or animals is rare. I would preach so that no man in my mountains would ever have to know my sorrow, for death is the most useless of all gifts which a man can give another. It solves nothing which could not be solved by peaceful means. Take Yuree the Mad. What gained she by death? Only her own. Thus she did not live to enjoy the pain she gave me, if that was her plan.

I would speak with all family heads. I planned my speech as the voice said "Hold" and the lights were still and there was a quietness in my cave of games.

"My people," I would say. "I know the horrors of war. For Logan the Unwise donned the bearclaws and came to raid my family and gained death, and I do not rejoice in his death, but know a deep sadness that the hills are depeopled and a family is in disaster. So heed my words. I ask all to toss the bear claws of war into the campfire and dance joy while they burn and thus banish the thought of war, of man killing man, from our customs forever and forever."

With my pain, I felt, I could make them see.

But now I was playing the game and coming to the end, and the eyes were blinking and showing picture after picture of tall and silent killbirds, and there came

to me a feeling of goodness. I thought that I had begun
to divine a meaning to this game. It was, after all, a
gift from God and not something left by a mythical
race of giants, and God was telling me something by
showing me images of so many of his messengers. He
was saying, the earth is for man, Eban the Hunter. It is
for man to live upon and feed well and bear and rear
his children, and in the end there is purpose, for if
there were not would I, your God, be showing you my
power in the form of the killbirds?

And so God spoke to me and I played the game and
prayed, and miracle of miracles I knew and understood. God was sending me messages.

The last of the game came, and with a sigh I pressed
the little blood-red thing and there was a click and the
voice begain to wail like a dozen dying lions and on the
eyes there was movement. The eyes blinked wildly and
in image after image the sleek and deadly killbirds began to move. Fire swirled from their tails and the
movement was upward, slowly, so slowly, as the eyes
blinked and switched and killbird after killbird lifted.
And I looked at the fanciful eye which looked down
upon a fanciful earth and lo, there were lances of fire
reaching upward.

It all happened with a swiftness which stunned me
and left me in awe. There were so many things to see.
Eyes showed my valley as if I were flying over it and
the valley was falling away, and one eye which caught
my notice showed a white streak in the sky, and I
shouted, for there was a killbird of the type I knew,
and it came with the speed of an evil thought, and
other eyes showed the white streak, which became a
gleaming and fatal killbird closing on one of the killbirds which I'd been watching, and they came together
and there was a flash of fire and, oh, there was so
much to watch. I could not see it all. I had views of my
valley falling away, views of a sky which soon began to
go black, and I could see on some eyes the huge array

of killbirds climbing on lances of fire straight up and the action was so swift that my head was jerking from side to side as I tried to take it all in, tried to see all the eyes at once.

What was the message? It came to me in a flash. God had heard Eban the Hunter and, although he had chosen to punish his servant by taking away the woman he loved most, was now rewarding his servant with a gift.

God would not give man wings unless he intended man to use them! God was sending his giant killbirds to destroy the gods of man, the sleek and small killbirds who lurked in the clean skies lying in wait to blast man on his wings.

"Thank you, thank you," I prayed, still watching. "Would it be too much to ask you, to beg you, God of all, to pull the teeth of all the dragons?"

I could not then count the vast number of huge killbirds which went aloft to do battle with the gods of man. I estimated sixty, seventy. The battle was a great one, God's killbirds smashing and destroying each other there high in the skies, and although I knew that it was not real, that it was a fanciful creation for my benefit on the eyes of the game thing, there was a feeling of joy in me, for it was God's way of telling me that now the skies, as the earth, were man's to enjoy.

I longed to leave, to join my family and to tell Yorerie and Cree to start building wings. We would fly! Oh, how we would soar and not fear the swift and deadly dart of a killbird, for God was destroying them. So many died at the meeting with God's giant killer killbirds that there could be none left to harass man in his feeble attempts to fly.

And now the view on the eyes was of a great blackness and a few stars and a funny ball below with mantles of stuff which seemed somewhat like clouds and a vast blueness. Another sign from God. He was showing me an image of the field of endless waters which his spirit warnings had prevented me from seeing during our travels in the far east. Of course it was not the real thing, for it was so far below and so tiny and curved on that funny ball.

Things remained the same for a period, and I stayed with my eyes on the many eyes. Then the views started to change and the ball below began to fill the eyes until the field of endless waters was lost from view and there were, below, mountains and plains, and they came toward me on the eyes, and then I looked at the eye which, throughout it all, had remained static and saw streaks moving downward, as if seeing the flight of killbirds from out in the heavens where God lives. And other eyes showed the killbirds as their noses grew red with anger and then split and out came dozens of little killbirds which left little tails of white as they flew. Had I been wrong? God's giants were giving birth to little killbirds? Had his message been misunderstood?

But no. God gave me still another sign. The small killbirds flew down, down, and then the fanciful land shown on the one eye which did not change bloomed with light and perfectly formed clouds swelled up from the earth in a blossoming of such beauty that my eyes stung with it and I wept tears of joy as I saw God's sign that all was well. He was creating chaos, which He loves, to show me that I had understood His message. And then I watched as one by one the eyes went blank, leaving only the unchanging eye which showed the clouds climbing, climbing, and then God spoke to me.

His voice was deep, and sometimes I could not be sure I was understanding, for a mere man is not expected to, nor can he hope to understand everything God says.

Afterward, I tried to use what I had learned in the read game to record the words of God in the symbols, but I was unsure, and so I depend mostly on memory. God said something like this.

"Now it is truly ended," God said.

Ah, I thought, I was right.

"Now we have won."

God and I, fighting the killbirds?

"Your presence here, man, your ability to follow instructions, shows that we have won, but your actions now have assured it. If you survived, some of them could have survived, and now your actions, well done, have made it possible to strike the final blow. Now the earth is yours, man. Now you must go forth, leave this place, for it has served its purpose. Go forth and populate the earth and tell your children of this time when you struck the final blow which gave victory, for if they did survive, they cannot come back, not in ten thousand years, from this final and devastating blow. And now, from the past, I wish you well, man. Remember us, your ancestors, and do not repeat our mistakes."

I waited. There was nothing more. I puzzled. God was my ancestor? I didn't know. I knew only that God had spoken and had left us one fine gift, the gift of the skies. I watched and the final eye went dead and the game things went to sleep and I left the room. The plate closed behind me, never to open again. I went into the valley to find my family still in mourning, but there was an air of excitement, and, indeed, great fear. They ran to me.

"Killbirds, killbirds," Yorerie yelled. "By the countless numbers."

It took me a long time to calm them down. And as they told me their stories I began to realize that it had not all been a creation of the eyes, but that God had actually come to earth and moved and that the death of the killbirds was not fanciful but real.

"I was walking," said Roden, pairmate of Cree, "with my children and the ground suddenly shook beneath my feet. Trees began to lean, and I ran. I looked back and the trees fell and the earth opened in a giant mouth."

It was no lie. We found the hole, and it was huge, lined with dragonskin, empty. There were, as we counted over the days which followed, an even one hundred of those holes, spread around our valley. (As time went on the rains and snows filled the killbird holes with water and they made fine swimming places for our young, although we discouraged it, since the water therein was so frightfully deep.)

"And then," Roden said, "there was a roar as of endless summer thunder, and as I feared for my life a giant killbird rose on a tail of fire, and I looked around—"

"They came from everywhere," Cree the Kite said excitedly, "so many we could not count, and the air was filled with their thunder, and—"

"I was so close," said Ouree, "that I could feel the heat of the tail of fire, and the force of his passing upward sent me sprawling to the ground."

"Thank God you were not hurt," I said.

"The air was filled with them," Yorerie said. "As many as the birds of the end of the summer, flying upward, and then the gods of man came and did battle with them and sent many of them from the sky." (Pieces of dragonskin fell into the village of Stoneskull, but hurt no one, giving Stoneskull's people material for many arrow heads and hardaxes.)

And so I listened to my family. All had seen and heard. It was a real thing. One hundred killbirds had risen from our valley to do battle with the gods of man. I was right. So many could not help but destroy all, and my knowledge of such things made me believe that killbirds, like dragons, did not breed, so that now the sky must be empty.

"My family," I said. "I have heard the voice of God. He has told me, Eban the Hunter, that the earth is ours and that the sky is ours, for His purpose in this wondrous thing was to kill the killbirds so that man can forever and in safety praise God with the wings which God gave him."

"Can it be true?" Yorerie, who once risked his life with no hope of gain merely to be able to make a long soar, was looking at the sky with a rapt expression.

"God has spoken to me," I said. "Although I still mourn, I will come out of mourning and we will build wings and we will praise Him with a flight . . ." I looked around and chose the highest hill. ". . . from that peak to the center of the valley."

"Ha, Eban," Yorerie yelled in joy.

We built in haste, but with care, for wings are not thrown together lightly. A support breaks in midair and a man tumbles to his death. We had an ample store of dragon's veins for tying, and the women worked to scrape the hides to a thinness, and at last they were ready. Then we three hunters, last of the Strabo family, climbed the hill, careful to stay inside the teeth-spitting range of the hill dragons, and cleared a place, making God's chaos in praise. On the morning we lifted after a run and we soared. Our valley made a nice cup for the creation of updrafts, and we went high, I confident yet keeping an eye on the sky to see the first hint of the white streak of a killbird. None came.

"Ha, Eban," Yorerie yelled in joy, swooping past me on a wing. I dived after him, chased him, yelled my joy. Cree came and zoomed past my head and I found an updraft and climbed and forgot that there ever had been such a thing as a killbird. We flew until the updrafts failed, and we landed, one after the other, on the meadow beside the stream to greet our family, who sang in joy. Nothing would do Yorerie but to make a second flight, so we trudged to the hill and ran and soared.

There were, needless to say, many flights of praise in the following time, and then a strange thing happened.

It was during the period when there was in the very air a strange tingle, a warning, the spirits talking to our bare bellies. It gave me some concern, but it was not strong, not deadly. Still, I knew not why there was warning in land which had always been safe until, consulting the Seer of Things Unseen, I was told that in our legends the old ones spoke of a time when the spirits of evil moved in the air. I doubted God, then. Had He given us one boon only to curse us in the giving? But in days the spirit was so low that one had to concentrate to feel it, and then it faded, and during that time we had no rain.

But while our attentions were on the spirits in the air and we were troubled, Ouree the Unclaimed built a pair of wings, copying them from ours, and announced her intentions of flying.

"Women do not fly," I said.

"I have consulted the Seer," Ouree said. She could be the most stubborn woman upon occasion, as I had found, since she tended my daughter, Margan, and the child I had fathered with her, whom she had named Mar. "There is nothing in our custom which says a woman cannot fly."

"But women have never flown," I said.

"We will consult the Seer," she said, with tight lips.

"Women are not strong enough to fight the winds of the sky," I said.

"I am strong enough to carry a deer," she said. "Can you say more?"

Well, a wise family head, indeed, a wise man, knows when he has no argument. I yielded and, to prevent the breaking of frail female bones, gave Ouree flight lessons, sitting on her desire to leap from the high hill and forcing her to take short and quickly ended glides from low places. She did well, damaging her wings on landing only once. The day came when nothing would do but for Ouree to fly from a high hill, though not the highest. I talked with her at length, warning her of the updrafts and the winds and giving her lessons in how to handle them, and then, white-faced, she ran and leaped and soared beautifully, her bare legs gleaming and her graceful form hanging below the wings in the saddle, and I heard her cry out in joy as she caught the updraft and circled.

"Do not climb high," I yelled at her. "Glide slowly toward the meadow."

"Beautiful," she yelled. "So beautiful."

And she climbed, the silly female. She went into the air and got the wind off the far hills.

"Dive, dive," I yelled at her. She was being swept slowly toward the rim of hills to the west. "Dive down and get below the hills!" But she was beyond the reach of my voice. I could see the people in the meadow below, and they were waving and shouting and I was shouting, and Ouree was still being swept toward the far rim. She was high.

I watched. "All right," I said, speaking as if she could hear me. "You have gone too far and now you cannot come back into the valley. Stay high, clear the hills. Above all, do not go down within range of the teeth of the dragons. Fly beyond the hills, find a meadow, land, and then fold your wings and walk back, coming all the way around."

Surely, surely, she was wise enough to know her danger. Surely. But she was now realizing her position and was trying to dive back. She was diving for the top of the hill where the dragons were rooted. Then, as I screamed and yelled, unseen and unheard, she came to her senses, soared and disappeared beyond the hills.

I made haste down the hill and found the family concerned. "Yorerie," I said, "you and I. We will go through the dragon's hole and march to meet her. Since we know not where she landed, nor if she will circle to the south or the north, one will go to the south and the other to the north, and we will meet her."

"How will I know when to turn back if I do not meet her?" Yorerie asked.

"I have been thinking of extending our range," I said. "It will be good if you scout all the way around the southern hills to a point directly to the west and then return by another route."

"Yes. You will do the same to the north?"

"I will," I said. "We take note of game signs, of water, of living sites, of fruit and nut trees."

"I will," Yorerie said.

We made preparation. I was worried about Ouree, but she was a solid-minded woman, skilled in the hunt, could be expected to be able to forage on the land for the few days it would take her to walk back around the hills. My only worry was that the land to the north and west had not been explored and there could be more dragons.

I thought of Ouree facing a dragon alone, and I was sick inside. Mar had loved her so. She was so gentle and so considerate, and she looked after our children, Margan and Mar, so well. But she would be fine, I told myself.

Old Seer would tend the two little girls. I would find Ouree in the wilderness and bring her back. Mar would have wanted that. And thinking of Mar I felt a little surge inside me. Woman. My Mar.

Mar, Mar, I said silently, can you understand why I fear so for the safety of Ouree? It is only because you loved her so, my Mar.

And as I set out beside the sturdy and dependable Yorerie to fetch back the young woman we'd both loved during the time she lived in the warm cave with us, I could see Mar's face smiling at me with a knowing look in her eyes.

Behind us the family waved. Then we were alone, and I heard or felt something, something I'd never heard or felt before, and, fearfully, I looked up.

Ref: Z-333-469-123-P-222

X&A Restriction Code 2

Origin: Minutes Board of Determination, Sector
          Lightning, Headquarters X&A, Mercer.

Sub.:   III Planet, Life Zone Class Xanthos II
          sun, sector Sub-Lightning 30-60-97-38.
          Inhabited Humanoid.

Dated: N.Y. 30,500, Month 4, day 24

Pres.:   Prof. Anton Bradley Gore.

The meeting was called to order by Chairman
Prof. Anton Bradley Gore. Prof. Gore announced
that the purpose of the Board of Determination
was to discuss the discovery of Class 1-A-sub Hu-
manoids, C-Scale primitive, T rating T-1. The
purpose of the meeting thus established, the
Chairman distributed copies of a report from
U.P.X. *Old Earth*, Capt. T. Willis, Cmmd. A
recess was called to allow the board to study the
report.

Upon reconvening, Chairman Gore called for
introductions by the individual board members.
The makeup of the board is as follows:

Chariman Gore: Some of you may question
my being chosen as chairman. If you do, I can't
blame you, for this is pretty high terrain for a
teacher of literature at Xanthos University. I sup-

pose I was selected since I was called upon, because of my specialty in alien literature, to analyze the hypnoprobe material gathered by members of the crew of the *Old Earth*. Since I taught the subject, I suppose they decided to use me. You know how those X&A fellows are about aliens. But since my duty is just to preside, I guess I'm as good as anyone, and I won't let any of my uneducated ideas intrude into your thinking. Now if you will stand, beginning with the Admiral, and introduce yourselves.

Admiral of Fleet Talltree the Healer: You are overly modest, professor. We've all read your astute theory of the Dead Worlds and your analysis of the Miaree legend. Speaking for myself, I say that I know of no man better qualified to deal with the alien mind. As for myself, I am a Fleet man, entered the Fleet as a mere boy and have served it since, primarily in exploration and alien search. It is quite obvious to all that I am a man of old earth, a healer. I have visited the planet in question and may be able, as this discussion goes along, to give some insight into the inhabitants.

Degan the Far Seer: I am here from my post at the observatory on Lightning because I was the only Far Seer willing to leave his job.

Moil the Power Giver: I don't know exactly why I'm here, except that such boards are made up, traditionally, of each of the three old earth types and an equal number of you New Ones.

Prof. Gore: Moil is being modest in her turn. She was my student, and a brilliant one. She, too, was on the planet. Next, please.

Capt. T. Willis: I was in command of the U.P.X. *Old Earth* when disturbances were noted on a planet of the core star now called Tom Thumb.

Prof. Gore: Somewhat facetiously, I must say. And now our U.P. representatives.

Ambassador John Zees: I am here because I was on a tour of the Lightning sector planets and was handy.

Prof. Gore: Ah, a general modesty seems to be the rule. Let me say that Ambassador Zees is a man who is outstanding in many fields. He is a scholar and a scientist who has worked on the Brett Drive project. He has traveled possibly as much or more than any other living man and knows our United Planets as well as any man. He was a member of the Board of Determination in the Dead Worlds inquiry and his thinking was largely responsible for my theory regarding the events there.

Secretary Anne Barker: Well, I won't be modest. I'm Secretary of U.P. Sector Lightning and damned proud of it, being the highest-ranked woman in the U.P. But I will stick to business and won't ask you to vote for me in the coming U.P. Presidential elections.

Prof. Gore: Madam Secretary, you already have my vote, so you don't have to ask for it. And now that we're acquainted and you've read the remarkable manuscript which was the result of hypnoprobe on a most curious planet, I'd like to turn teacher for a moment and give you a few of my thoughts.

We live in a remarkable time. In just a few hundred years events of singular importance have occurred. First there was the reunion of the two branches of our race with the discovery of our native world and of our remote ancestors, who had changed a bit—

Adm. Talltree the Healer: To put it mildly.

Prof. Gore: —and for the better: the Healer with his ability to cure cells and improve the

health of both branches of the race. the Power
Giver with her remarkable gifts of levitation; the
Far Seer with his greatly advanced mind which
has helped the race to advance and which deals
best with pure theory and opens up endless fields
for exploration. This reunion, in itself, changed
the course of human events. And, for the first
time, it gave purpose to a rather neglected branch
of the service known as X&A, Exploration and
Alien Search. We Old Ones, or mere humans,
who left the old earth and forgot our origin, were
slightly xenophobic, and with good reason, for before the reunion, we had discovered the grim and
terrible destruction of those planets which became
known as the Dead Worlds, and we had come
face to face with evidence of alien presence, at
least in the past, and a power which could gut and
kill entire planets.

The discovery of true aliens, beings with some
pretty impressive psi powers, even though they
turned out to be the original race of man mutated
following a thermonuclear war on old earth, and
the presence of the Dead Worlds, and the return of
X&A ships from the colliding galaxies in Cygnus
with the remarkable manuscript which has become known as the Legend of Miaree—all served
to warn us, and to frighten some of us. We saw
the possibility of other life somewhere in our uni-
verse, even in our own galaxy, for the size of it is
not yet comprehended even by the most astute
of us.

Until a few months ago, we knew of four races.
Ourselves, counting both branches as one; the
Dead Worlders, who were indeed deadly, leaving
nothing to hint at their nature save their savagery;
and the two races of the colliding galaxies. Now
all races have shown a remarkable tendency
toward one activity, and that activity is killing

each other. The Dead Worlds are indeed dead, and the events of the Dead Worlds Expedition of LaConious of Tigian, which made discoveries still quite puzzling to us, served to reemphasize the threat which still hangs over man. The two remarkable humanoid races of the Cygnus galaxies died in mutual destruction. Old earth was ravaged by war. It is saddening to me to realize that of all known races in our univese—of course, there may be and most probably are others which we have not yet encountered—none to our knowledge has lived in peace with itself.

It is this aspect of the new encounter with an alien species which, I feel, must occupy much of our thought. Why are intelligent species warlike? Why do they belie their intelligence and, in the case of the Dead Worlds and the Cygnus civilizations, destroy themselves, or as in the case of old earth, ruin a planet and almost wipe out a race?

I hope that each of you has studied the available information, especially the hypnoprobe material dealing with the story of Eban the Hunter. Ha—I find myself addressing you as students. Now, to add to our understanding, I think a description of the planet and its people and an account of events would be instructive. Admiral Talltree?

Adm. Talltree the Healer: To keep things in order, I call upon Captain Willis, who was in command of the nearest X&A ship when detection of activity was made on the planet called Tom Thumb.

Capt. Willis: We were on a routine probe on the outskirts of Lightning Sector. Detection was made by our Far Seer. He sensed thermonuclear radiation coming from a source which was not a natural star, and I blinked back to headquarters for permission to investigate. We went in after taking all precautions. As you say, Professor Gore, we all remember the Dead Worlds and the old earth, and newks popping off makes my hair stand on edge. We found a life-zone planet circling a Xanthos II type sun, a three planet, as are most life-zone planets, and our instruments measured considerable radiation, concentrated on one landmass. We sent down a Healer and he reported back that it was pretty hot, too hot even for him with his radiation resistance, and that the populace, apparently a stone-age culture living in a devastated land which had once before been reduced by newks, was dying by the hundreds. I say hundreds only because that was the number of people. The landmass was quite thinly populated by nomadic tribes. The salvo of newks—our officer estimated over two hundred hits in the ten-megaton range using high neutron radiation—had blanketed the entire landmass. It seemed strange as hell to us for a salvo of heavy newks to be targeted at a landmass peopled by stone-age men. We started a search for the origin of the salvo and found radiation levels to be much lower on the other large landmass of the planet, but the winds aloft were carrying the residue of the salvo over and it was pretty hot. We sent down Lieutenant Moil to take a look, and she reported back that the landmass was thickly peopled, with concentrations in the mountainous areas.

I knew I had something. Those were men down there, even if they were pygmies, or dwarfs. They were about thirty inches in height and they lived in sort of stone age with some tools fashioned of metal from the scraps left by a highly technological culture. But they were men. So I held off and waited for a team headed by Admiral Talltree to arrive.

Adm. Talltree the Healer: As is the rule, we

did not make overt contact with the aliens. My team, consisting of myself, Moil the Power Giver and Lieutenant Elk the Healer, member of the *Old Earth's* crew, made observations, and after several days of overflight, using instruments, we found the source of the salvo. There were one hundred launch silos in a small valley in the heart of the mountains. Surprisingly, there was a tribe of the small people living there, and they gave us some surprises. They used hang gliders and flew, and they lived there with those one hundred silos as if they didn't even mind them. And they had to have seen the launch. Our big question was, who fired those missiles?

We rigged a protective ship for the *Old Earth's* Far Seer and took him down into the valley. We picked a time when the entire tribe was gathered so that the Far Seer's mind could control all of them. At the end of Eban's tale you can see where we entered, and the Far Seer's mind took over. After that it was simple. We merely probed all of them. We found that the leader, who called himself Eban the Hunter, knew more than the others, so their stories were not presented to this board.

Thus, from Eban, we learned that he himself had launched the strike on the other landmass with no idea of what he had done. It was a diabolical thing, the way those people, who from what we were able to learn must have been humanoid and very much like the Old Ones of our race, reached up from their graves and coaxed Eban into killing more people than he'd ever seen, people he didn't even know existed. Revenge from the grave. Having wiped each other out, returning themselves to a stone age, the dying ones rigged the complex. Their thinking must have been colored by the knowledge that they were dying, that their entire race was wiped out and that only mutants or severely weakened members would survive. And they reached up from the grave to smite the poor mutated remnants of their enemies and, as "God" told Eban, to give the earth to their own mutated descendants.

We searched, using the most delicate instruments and all the senses of Power Giver, Far Seer and Healer, to find other hidden missiles, and there were none. Only the people of Eban's landmass had seen into the future and the possibility of one last blow at the enemy.

Prof. Gore: Thank you, admiral. I'd like some general observations now. It is my conclusion that Eban's people are basically peaceful. Any comment?

Sec. Anne Barker: To me, Eban showed a great potential for violence. He killed two "inbreeders" without qualms—

Moil the Power Giver: Pardon me. He did have qualms. He regretted it.

Sec. Anne Barker: He was the stronger. He could have overpowered them without killing them. And he could certainly have overpowered the woman, Yuree, rather than kill her with an ax. No. I think he showed primitive tendencies toward violence, and it is my contention that his race is several thousand years away from being developed into civilized beings.

Moil the Power Giver: He abolished death. He resolved to preach peace to all his people. I think he is gentle and sensitive and worth contacting.

Degan the Far Seer: That brings us to the central issue. Contact or no? At this level of development I am not sure contact would be beneficial to Eban's people. As I understand it they have a certain resistance to the levels of radioactivity on the planet. It is unfortunate that we did not discover them in time to prevent the last salvo of thermonuclear weapons, which killed so many, but we did not. We can in no way hold Eban responsible for that. The question is, is Eban the result, the product, of a race with built-in killer senses? Would he—of course, I speak of his race in general—become a useful part of the U.P., or would the killer come out in him in the future? Together, using the lesson of old earth as an example, we have abolished war, and such is our society that even individual killings are extremely rare. Would Eban's people bring back to our society, as the integration took place and they were advanced to our level of education and technology, the kill syndrome?

Amb. John Zees: One question, please. I simply wonder if Eban's people have the intelligence to become part of our society.

Prof. Gore: I call your attention to the extent of Eban's vocabulary. Of course, you have all read a translation, but I assure you, as somewhat of an expert on language, that his language is rich, varied and quite expressive. Much was retained—no technological words, of course—from the original language. The race also retained the art of counting, and Eban quickly learned numbers, simple arithmetic and even basic reading. Yes, I think he shows a basic intelligence and an ability to learn.

Sec. Anne Barker: So the question is twofold. One, would it be best for Eban's people? Two, would contact be in the best interest of the U.P?

Adm. Talltree: I remind myself that man has always felt lonely, has spent much of his energy and his resources in the search for other intelligent beings. Eban's people fit the discription.

Moil the Power Giver: Eban's people are fairly happy. They live well, by primitive standards. Given a choice, I'm not sure whether they would desert their way of life, their customs. But I think of the others, the ones Eban calls the inbreeders, living in the devastated areas, without Eban's gift of sensing deadly radiation. They could be helped.

Degan the Far Seer: True. The lifespan of an inbreeder is about twenty-five old years. Only the fact that their reproduction systems seem to have been affected toward multiple births keeps their population static. Over half the births are malformed and are killed without question. There is widespread cancer. But with the residues of radiation firmly planted in their bodies, it would take generations to breed a clean form.

Moil the Power Giver: One problem has been solved, probably without your knowledge, Degan. It is now possible to leach the long-lasting radioactives from bone marrow. Indeed, we dosed Eban's daughter, Margan, with the leaching agent while she was under hypno. It would take a massive effort, but many of the inbreeders could be saved, and a generation without radioactives would result.

Capt. T. Willis: If we can do that I think we'd be less than human if we didn't help them.

Sec. Anne Barker: Such a program would require a life-zone planet, massive removals, huge medical expenses. Should it be decided to move the population without their knowledge, under hypno, the expenses would be staggering.

Moil the Power Giver: So we just forget them, let them continue to die of hunger, cancer, radiation sickness?

Sec. Anne Barker: I have merely stated the facts.

Adm. Talltree: There is one other aspect of the problem. If we should decide to do anything, what would be done with the "monsters" which Eban encountered in the east? We saw those beings. They're mutants. Once man. They're man-like, and they're horrible. Even more horrible in appearance than a Healer or a Far Seer.

Prof. Gore: But are they human?

Adm. Talltree: I was in the thoughts of one. Low level of intelligence, say like a domestic dog. But human in form. They know pain and hunger and lust.

Prof. Gore: Nothing is ever simple. We have three phases of this problem: Eban's people, the inbreeders, the mutants.

Sec. Anne Barker: I'm as human as anyone, but I don't see why we have to concern ourselves with the mutants. I'm sure we don't have some magic agent to leach them into being healthy human beings.

Degan the Far Seer: I think I am ready to state my opinion. I would classify both Eban's people and the inbreeders as intelligent beings worthy of our help. I am not yet ready to state whether I advise open or covert contact, but I do advise you all that we have a responsibility, as fellow thinking beings with more advantages, to help the people of Tom Thumb. I would advise a further study on the scene, and a decision by a higher authority as to the direction and extent of our help, but it should certainly include medical attentions, however expensive.

Prof. Gore: Any further discussion? . . . There being none, we will hear the opinions, one by one.

Admiral Talltree: I endorse Degan's views.

Moil the Power Giver: And I, with one request. I request that I be assigned to the study team.

Capt. J. Willis: That Eban is quite a guy. Imagine a little runt like him going up against that thing which is translated as bear. That animal makes a Trajan bearcat look small, and he killed one with a spear. I don't think we could lose with people like Eban. I wouldn't mind having men like him in my crew, even if they are runts. I vote for study and help as quickly as possbile.

Amb. John Zees: While in general I am sympathetic to the view of Degan, I withhold my recommendation for the moment.

Sec. Barker: I go along with further study, with a definite limit on spending, and only covert contact.

Prof. Gore: Thank you, all of you. A copy of the minutes of this meeting and its recommendations will be forwarded by urgent blinkstat to U.P. headquarters, where final action will be decided upon. I, too, favor the views of Degan the Far Seer. There are many possibilities. The research activities on old earth have taught us much about cleaning up the lingering radiation of a nuclear war. Perhaps the U.P. Council might see fit to covertly lessen the radiation on Tom Thumb. I am not familiar with the costs of such an operation. Perhaps the population of the planet will be moved to another life-zone planet. But I am sure that something will be done.

Any further discussion? Meeting adjourned.

X&A Code Personal-Personal
Blink Priority Urgent-Personal

    Origin: Tom Thumb, Lightning Sector
    To: Prof. A. Bradley Gore
               Dept. of Liberal Education
               Xanthos University
               Xanthos, Sector Home L-1
    From: Lt. Moil the Power Giver

Knowing you, my dear and respected teacher, I'm sure that your curiosity is killing you, so I'm going to squander half a week's pay to bring you up to date on the story of Eban the Hunter.

First, thank you for your help in having me assigned to the study team. We've been on Tom Thumb for three months now. The radiation from the last salvo has settled, and it's very clean here now, with only traces of bad stuff. We're camped on the hills overlooking Eban's valley. We had to disable some of his "dragons" to move about freely, and we operate, of course, behind a hypnoshield.

These are fascinating little people. They're as brave as a Pharos lion. Eban killed a bear last week, but I'm getting ahead of my story.

The dragons are interesting. They are all that remains of the vast and complicated technology of the old civilization. This planet must have been a very rich one, for the noncorrosive metals are used heavily, platinum and gold and silver. The heavy armor is an alloy of steel which is interesting. It shows signs of rust—that's Eban's blood—but does not rust away, like ordinary steel or iron. We dismantled one dragon and found the electronics to be unimpressive but efficent. There is heavy use of rather antique resistors and capacitors. (Yes, as you guessed, the dragon's guts were, indeed, color-coded electronic components.)

After our study, we moved away from that dragon and left it, split open, for Eban's people to discover, and there was much happiness in the valley and now all of them wear necklaces of dragon's guts.

The population is growing rapidly. The windows—and, old dear, you goofed on that word, for I suspect the proper translation is "widow"—have exercised their rights, and to their "walkers" have been added a new crop of babies. It keeps Eban and the other two hunters busy, for after the salvo, the "cave" closed itself down, blew itself up, and buried the entrance, leaving the family to their own provisions. But game is plentiful and the family lives well.

The other half of the team, running tests in the low slopes, is having great success in leaching radioactives from the bone marrow of the inbreeders. An investigation of the "monsters" of the east reveals a new possibility—not man at all, but a mutated form of another and lower anthropoid. Their numbers are limited and their range is small, thus we are not faced with a large problem there.

It was interesting to me to find that the western half

of this landmass is totally devastated. Our archaeological teams are learning a little bit about the old civilization—very human, very tech, very deadly, very sick and now dead. A few art works have been recovered. They were very much like you Old Ones, but had a tendency toward, if you can believe the images, monstrous mammary glands in the female and bald heads in the men.

I'm doing this deliberately, old dear, knowing that you're burning to know about Eban, but knowing also that you won't cheat and look ahead.

Eban, poor thing, is sure that God brought another miracle, for in his mind just as he started away from the camp bound to search for Ouree, she came walking toward him, carrying her wings. There was, however, some confusion, and I have to report that our team goofed down here before.

This year is known to Eban as the Year Which Lost Three Days, for that's how long we kept the family under hypnoprobe, and the time totem, whereon the Seer of Things Unseen strikes off the passing days, does not agree with Ouree's passage of time, for she was walking home during those three days.

Moreover, Ouree arrived in the valley in time to see our scout lift off, and she told Eban that she saw God leave as she watched, and that God had been speaking to him. Thus, Eban is now considered a Holy Man, and, as he promised, went preaching peace to the surrounding families.

As for Eban himself, although he still grieves for his Mar, he is a man, with man's needs, and he has taken as pairmate the daughter of the Seer, once known as Ouree the Unclaimed and now called Ouree the Flyer, for she loves to hang-glide. She and Eban often climb the hill and fly.

Incidentally, we had to destroy a hunter-killer missile. All of them were not used up in the big battle of the salvo; at least one stray was left. We detected it coming, high, one day when the males of the family were soaring, and shot it down before they saw it. We made a probe of near space and found several dead satellites and a few hunter-killers which were malfunctioned and wiped them out, too.

During his travels preaching peace, Eban recruited three young males, and they have now pairmated with three of the "windows." The family prospers. The fame of Eban is spreading, and there have been two delegations from neighboring families come to hear his tales and to see the water-filled silos from which the killbirds flew. The futures of the children are assured, for alliances have been made. Margan is a lovely child and the leaching was successful. She has none of the "sickness" in her bones now and my only fear is that something went wrong in the process, for she shows signs of being near the size of an Old Onechild at her age, which makes her almost as big as her mother, or her stepmother, Ouree. Have we got a mutation back toward the original race of "giants"? The inbreeders showed signs of it, as did Eban, who was considered a freak among his people.

In my last report, I said that I have never known a more gentle and more likable people than these. I urge you to throw your support toward full contact, for I think they have the intelligence to accept us without fatal cultural shock. They're very adaptable, these little people.

And still, I have, especially alone in my bed at night,

some doubts, for I have seen the virulent sickness in the form of those dragons. The old race, in dying, fortified their land, and programmed their weapons to slay anything that moved, friend or foe. And the hunter-killer missiles, heat seekers, were so sensitive that we've found evidence, in the form of wreckage and animal remains, that they would attack large birds. There must have been thousands of them originally, for the large-bird population of the landmass is nonexistent.

There are many things to be learned here, and I'm sure studies will go on forever before a decision is made. For example, a scientific team just arrived whose sole mission is to find out how a semblance of technology, in the form of the hang gliders, survived the cataclysm. Experiments are going on in cleaning up radiation, and they're practical, if expensive, for they allow our teams to operate in the highly radioactive areas along the two oceans where the old population was concentrated. I will keep you informed, and I ask the same of you, you being near U.P. center and able to keep up to date with the sometimes wise and sometimes not so wise action of the politicians.

I am out of time and will have to save the story of Eban's bear, killed to give Ouree a warm bed, for the next blinkstat.

ZACH HUGHES is the pen name of Hugh Zachary, who, with his wife, Elizabeth, runs a book factory in North Carolina. Hugh quit a timeclock job in 1963 and turned to writing full-time. Since then Hugh and Elizabeth have turned out many fine historical romances together, as well as books in half a dozen other fields.

While turning out 87 books, Hugh Zachary also worked in radio and tv broadcasting and as a newspaper feature writer. He has also been a carpenter, run a charter fishing boat, done commercial fishing, and served as a mate on an anchor handling tugboat in the North Sea oil fields.

Among his science fiction titles are: *Seed of the Gods, Gwen, in Green, The Book of Rack the Healer,* and *The Legend of Miaree.*

SIGNET Science Fiction You'll Enjoy

☐ **STARBURST by Alfred Bester.** (#E9132—$1.75)*
☐ **THE REBEL WORLDS by Poul Anderson.** (#E9046—$1.75)
☐ **A CIRCUS OF HELLS by Poul Anderson.** (#E9045—$1.75)
☐ **DANCER FROM ATLANTIS by Poul Anderson.**
(#W7806—$1.50)
☐ **BEYOND THE BEYOND by Poul Anderson.** (#W7760—$1.50)
☐ **THE DAY OF THEIR RETURN by Poul Anderson.**
(#W7941—$1.50)
☐ **PEOPLE OF THE WIND by Poul Anderson.** (#W7900—$1.50)
☐ **EYE AMONG THE BLIND by Robert Holdstock.**
(#E8480—$1.75)
☐ **A SMALL ARMAGEDDON by Mordecai Roshwald.**
(#W7194—$1.50)†
☐ **THE BEAST THAT SHOUTED LOVE AT THE HEART OF THE WORLD by Harlan Ellison.** (#E8590—$1.75)
☐ **APPROACHING OBLIVION by Harlan Ellison.**
(#W7718—$1.50)
☐ **ELLISON WONDERLAND by Harlan Ellison.** (#W7717—$1.50)
☐ **MOONSTAR ODYSSEY by David Gerrold.** (#W7372—$1.50)
☐ **SECRETS OF STARDEEP by John Jakes.** (#W8237—$1.50)
☐ **TIME GATE by John Jakes.** (#Y7889—$1.25)

* Price slightly higher in Canada
† Not available in Canada